HARLEQUIN®
Presents

What have we got for you in Harlequin Presents books this month? Some of the most gorgeous men you're ever likely to meet!

With *His Royal Love-Child*, Lucy Monroe brings you another installment in her gripping and emotional trilogy, ROYAL BRIDES; Prince Marcello Scorsolini has a problem—his mistress is pregnant! Meanwhile, in Jane Porter's sultry, sexy new story, *The Sheikh's Disobedient Bride*, Tally is being held captive in Sheikh Tair's harem...because he intends to tame her! If it's a Mediterranean tycoon that you're hoping for, Jacqueline Baird has just the guy for you in *The Italian's Blackmailed Mistress*: Max Quintano, ruthless in his pursuit of Sophie, whom he's determined to bed using every means at his disposal! In Sara Craven's *Wife Against Her Will*, Darcy Langton is stunned when she finds herself engaged to businessman Joel Castille— traded as part of a business merger! The glamour continues with *For Revenge...Or Pleasure?*—the latest title in our popular miniseries FOR LOVE OR MONEY, written by Trish Morey, truly is romance on the red carpet! If it's a classic read you're after, try *His Secretary Mistress* by Chantelle Shaw. She pens her first sensual and heartwarming story for the Presents line with a tall, dark and handsome British hero, whose feisty yet vulnerable secretary tries to keep a secret about her private life that he won't appreciate.

Check out www.eHarlequin.com for a list of recent Presents books! Enjoy!

Bedded by... *Blackmail*

Forced to bed...then to wed?

He's got her firmly in his sights and she's got only one chance of survival—surrender to his blackmail...and him...in his bed!

Bedded by... **Blackmail**

The *big* miniseries from Harlequin Presents®.

Dare you read it?

Jacqueline Baird

THE ITALIAN'S BLACKMAILED MISTRESS

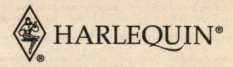

Bedded by... *Blackmail*
Forced to bed...then to wed?

HARLEQUIN®

TORONTO • NEW YORK • LONDON
AMSTERDAM • PARIS • SYDNEY • HAMBURG
STOCKHOLM • ATHENS • TOKYO • MILAN • MADRID
PRAGUE • WARSAW • BUDAPEST • AUCKLAND

ISBN 0-373-12543-7

THE ITALIAN'S BLACKMAILED MISTRESS

First North American Publication 2006.

Copyright © 2006 by Jacqueline Baird.

This edition published by arrangement with Harlequin Books S.A.

® and TM are trademarks of the publisher. Trademarks indicated with ® are registered in the United States Patent and Trademark Office, the Canadian Trade Marks Office and in other countries.

www.eHarlequin.com

Printed in U.S.A.

All about the author...
Jacqueline Baird

JACQUELINE BAIRD was born and raised in Northumbria, U.K. She met her husband when she was eighteen. Eight years later, after many adventures around the world, she came home and married him. They still live in Northumbria and have two grown-up sons.

Jacqueline's number one passion is writing. She has always been an avid reader and she had her first success as a writer at the age of eleven, when she won first prize in the Nature Diary of the Year competition at school. But she always felt a little guilty because her diary was more fiction than fact.

She always loved romance novels and when her sons went to school all day, she thought she would try writing one. She's been writing for the Harlequin Presents line ever since, and she still gets a thrill every time a new book is published.

When Jacqueline is not busy writing, she likes to spend her time traveling, reading and playing cards. She was a keen sailor until a knee injury ended her sailing days, but she still enjoys swimming in the sea when the weather allows.

She visits a gym three times a week and has made the surprising discovery that she gets some good ideas while doing the mind-numbingly boring exercises on the cycling and weight machines.

CHAPTER ONE

MAXIMILIAN ANDREA QUINTANO—Max to his friends—
walked out of the bathroom wearing only a pair of navy
silk boxer shorts. Just the effort of bending to pull them
on had made his head spin. He needed air and, walking out
onto the balcony that ran the length of the suite, he willed
the pain behind his eyes to vanish. It was his own fault. It
had been his thirty-first birthday two days ago, and
although Max owned a penthouse in Rome and a house in
Venice, he had done what was expected of him and spent
the day at the family estate in Tuscany with his father, stepmother, Lisa, and other family members.

But on his return to Rome yesterday, after he had taken
his yearly medical exam for insurance purposes, he'd met
up with his best friend Franco and a few others from his
university days for lunch. The party that had ensued had
ended up with Franco belatedly remembering his wife
was expecting him home in Sicily. Max, due to fly there
the next day anyway, had agreed to accompany Franco to
the island to carry on the party there.

Finally, at four-thirty in the morning and feeling much
the worse for wear, Max had got a taxi to the Quintano

Hotel, the hotel he was scheduled to arrive at that same afternoon in place of his father.

Ever since Max's grandfather had built his first hotel on the island, before relocating the family to Tuscany, it had become a tradition for the Quintano family to holiday at the Sicilian hotel during the month of August. For the last decade Max had rarely visited, leaving it to his brother Paulo and the rest of the family to carry on the tradition.

A deep frown suddenly creased Max's broad brow as he thought of his older brother's tragic death in a car accident just four months ago. When Paulo had enthusiastically entered the family business and become a top hotelier, Max had been given the freedom to pursue his own interests, and he knew he owed his brother a lot.

An adventurer at heart, Max had left university with a degree in geology, boundless energy and a rapier-sharp brain. He had headed to South America, where on his arrival, he'd acquired an emerald mine in a game of poker. Max had made the mine a success and started the MAQ Mining Corporation, which over the last nine years had expanded to include mines in Africa, Australia and Russia. The MAQ Corporation was now global, and Max was a multimillionaire in his own right. But, as he had been forcibly reminded a few months ago, all the money in the world could not solve every problem.

Deeply shocked and saddened by Paulo's death, Max had offered to help his father in any way he could with the hotel business. His father had asked him if he would check the running of the hotel in Sicily and stay a while to keep the tradition going. The loss of Paulo was too fresh for

Paulo's widow Anna and their young daughters to go, so of course Max had agreed.

Max rubbed his aching temples with his fingertips. The way he felt at the moment he was glad he had agreed to his father's request—he desperately needed the break. *Dios!* Never again, he vowed. By some miracle, when he'd arrived at the hotel just before dawn he had retained enough sense to instruct the night porter to keep his early arrival quiet. Nothing and no one was to disturb him….

Max stepped from the balcony into the sitting room. He needed coffee—black, strong and fast. He stopped dead.

For a moment he wondered if he was hallucinating.

A tall, feminine figure with a mass of flowers in her arms seemed to glide across the room towards him. Her hair was pale blond, and swept back into a long ponytail to reveal a face ethereal in its beauty. Her breasts he could only imagine, but her waist was emphasised by a black leather belt neatly holding a straight black skirt, which ended a few inches above her knees. The simple skirt revealed the seductive curve of her hips, and as for her legs… A sudden stirring in his groin said it all. She was gorgeous. *'Ciao, bella ragazza,'* he husked.

Sent up by the hotel manager to deposit the flowers and check the suite before the arrival of its illustrious owner, Sophie Rutherford was startled by the sound of the deep, masculine voice. She jerked her head towards the open French doors, the flowers falling from her hands at the sight of the huge man standing before her.

Frozen in shock, she swept her green gaze over him. Thick black hair fell over a broad brow, and dark, heavy-lidded eyes were set in a square-jawed, ruggedly handsome face. His bronzed muscular body was wide shouldered, with a broad chest lightly dusted with black hair that arrowed down over a flat stomach and disappeared beneath his dark shorts. His legs were long and splayed. He looked like some great colossus, she thought fancifully, and her green eyes widened in awe at so much masculine power.

Then he stepped towards her.... 'Oh, my God!' she cried, suddenly remembering where she was and belatedly realising he had no right to be there. 'Don't move! I'm calling Security.'

The scream echoed though Max's head like a razor on the bone. He closed his eyes for a second. The last thing he needed was someone calling the deity down on him. Then his less than sharp mind finally registered that her words had been spoken in English.

Max slowly opened his eyes, but before he could make a response she was disappearing out of the door. He heard the turn of the key in the lock behind her and could not believe it; the crazy girl had locked him in his own suite....

Shaking his head in amazement, he picked up the telephone and revealed his presence to Alex, the hotel manager. The he ordered some much needed coffee, and strode back into the bedroom to dress. Once he had shaved and dressed he returned to the sitting room, to find a maid cleaning away the flowers and Alex placing a coffee tray on the table. There was no mistaking the barely contained amusement in Alex's eyes as he greeted his old friend.

'Max, it's good to see you. I guessed you were the undesirable *giant* about to rob the place,' Alex said and he burst out laughing.

'Very funny, Alex. It's good to see you, too. Now, tell me, who the hell is the crazy girl?' Max asked, pouring himself a cup of coffee and downing it in one go, before collapsing onto one of the sofas.

'Sophie Rutherford,' Alex answered, joining Max on the sofa. 'Her father, Nigel Rutherford, is the owner of the Elite Agency in London. They handle the arrangements for a lot of our European clients, and Nigel asked me if his daughter could work here for a couple of months during her university vacation to improve her language skills. She is studying Russian and Chinese, but she also has a good grasp of Italian, French and Spanish. I thought, given the international clientele we attract, she could be very useful. She has certainly proved her worth already in the month she has been here. She is happy to work anywhere, and nothing is too much trouble for her.'

'If she is as good as you say, then I trust your judgement.' Max grinned at the older man. 'But my guess is the fact she is so beautiful might also have affected your decision,' he mocked.

'You would say that.' Alex grinned back. 'But, unlike you, it takes more than a pretty face to influence me—especially at my age.'

'Liar,' Max drawled, a knowing, sensual smile curving his hard mouth as the image of the young woman flashed up in his mind. 'Any man with breath in his body can see she is gorgeous, and I for one would like to get to know her a whole lot better.'

'Sophie is not for you, Max,' Alex said suddenly

serious. 'She is only nineteen, and in the absence of her father she is under my protection. Much as I like you, I do not think she is your kind of woman. She is serious about her studies and not the type of girl to have an affair—she is more the marrying kind.'

Max could have been insulted, but he wasn't. Alex was like an honorary uncle to him, and knew him well. As much as Max loved women, and they loved him, he had no intention of marrying for years—if ever. Since Paulo's death his father had begun to hint that it was time he married, constantly reminding Max that if he didn't there would be no male to carry on the great name of Quintano. But Max didn't want to settle down. He wanted to travel the world, doing what he loved. And with more money than he knew what to do with, Max was quite happy for Paulo's family to inherit their rightful share of his father's estate—as they naturally would have done if Paulo had lived. The last thing Max felt he needed was a wife.

'That's a shame.' His firm lips twisted wryly. 'She is delectable. But have no fear, old man, I promise not to seduce her. Now, shall we get down to business?'

Later that afternoon Max walked through the semicircle of trees that fringed the secure hotel beach and scrambled over the rocky headland to the small cove he had first discovered as a boy. He loved to dive from the rocks, and it was here that he had first become interested in geology. Today, however, the only rocks that concerned him were the ones in his skull, and he knew a swim would clear his head and cool him down.

Just then, a flash of pale gold against the backdrop of dark stone captured his attention. His dark eyes narrowed intently as he realised it was the girl from this morning. As he watched she flicked the shimmering mass of her hair over one shoulder and stretched herself out on a towel.

Silently Max moved towards her, his body reacting with instant masculine enthusiasm as his dark gaze swept over her. The pink bikini she was wearing was quite modest, compared to some he had seen, but the figure it graced was the ultimate in feminine allure. Her eyes were closed, and her glorious hair lay in a silken stream over one high firm breast. He had been right about her legs—they were long, slender and very sexy—and her skin was as smooth as silk, with just the shimmer of a tan. Max couldn't take his eyes off her, and he was instantly regretting his promise to Alex to leave her alone.

As he moved closer his shadow fell over her and she opened her eyes.

'Sophie Rutherford, I believe?' he drawled smoothly, and held out his hand. 'I am Max Quintano.' Max watched as she shot to her feet as though electrified. 'This morning did not seem to be quite the right time to introduce myself. Please forgive me for any embarrassment I may have caused you.' He smiled.

'Sophie, yes…' She blushed and took his hand. 'It is nice to meet you, Mr Quintano, but I think it is I who should apologise to you, for locking you in your room.'

Max felt the slight tremble in her hand and looked into her gorgeous green eyes. There he saw embarrassment, but also the feminine interest she could not hide—and miraculously his hangover vanished. 'Please, call me Max. There is no need to apologise—it was my fault—I must have startled you. Anyway, it is much too hot to argue, and as it happens you are occupying my favourite beach.' He smiled again. 'I wouldn't want to chase you away—I have already done that once today—please stay and allow me to show you that my apology is genuine and I am not some *giant* burglar.'

Sophie pulled her suddenly tingling hand from his and almost groaned. 'Did Alex tell you I said that? How embarrassing.'

Never before had she felt such instant and overwhelming attraction for a man. She had taken one look at him this morning and, shocked witless, had behaved like a terrified child.

Now, desperate to improve his impression of her, she added with a wry smile, 'But, in my defence, you really *are* very tall.'

'I'm six foot five—and there is no need for embarrassment, Sophie. I can assure you I am not in the least embarrassed by it. However, you do look rather red in the face—how about a swim to cool off?' Max suggested. Not giving her time to answer, he added, 'Race you to the water!'

Of course Sophie followed him. He hadn't doubted for a moment that she would; women had chased him all his adult life.

Wading into the water, Max turned and splashed her, and saw her smile broaden to light up her whole face. He also saw the gleam of mischief in her eyes just before she bent down and splashed him back.

The horseplay that followed did nothing to cool Max's suddenly rampant libido. Had she any idea that when she bent forward her lush breasts were bobbing up and down and almost out of her top? he wondered.

Eventually Max could stand it no longer, and he scooped her up into his arms. 'Trying to splash me, are you? You're going to pay for that, lady,' he declared, and waded farther out until the water lapped at his thighs.

'Don't you dare!' she cried, wrapping her arms firmly around Max's neck, her green eyes sparkling with laughter.

'There is nothing I wouldn't do to have you in my arms, Sophie,' Max teased, his dark gaze clashing with hers.

For a long moment their eyes locked, and the teasing stopped as desire, fierce and primitive, raced between them.

Sophie's green eyes darkened as for the first time in her life she felt the sudden rush of sexual desire for a man. She was intensely aware of Max's arm under her thighs, his other across her back and under her arm, the pressure of his long fingers splayed against the side of her breast. Her stomach churned and her pulse raced as the rest of the world seemed to stop. She simply stared into his eyes as though hypnotized, and the air between them grew heavy and shimmered with sexual tension.

Her gaze fell to his wide, firm mouth, and instinctively her lips parted as she imagined how his lips, his kiss, would feel.

The next second Sophie was under the water, swallowing what felt like half the ocean. Spluttering and gasping, she stood up and wiped the water from her eyes, to find Max watching her with a strange, almost regretful look on his face.

'I think we both need to cool off a little. I'm going to swim to the headland—see you later, Sophie.' And, like a sleek dolphin, Max dived out to sea, his strong brown arms cleaving the surface without so much as a ripple in the water.

Only later would she realise that a shark would have been a more appropriate metaphor....

Sophie watched him, helpless to do otherwise. Nothing in her nineteen years had prepared her for a man like Max Quintano.

After the death of her mother, when she was eleven, she had been sent to a girls' boarding school by her father. By the time she had reached the age of thirteen she had sprouted up like a beanpole to five feet nine and had become terribly self-conscious. She'd had few friends, and had spent the school holidays at home in Surrey, with Meg the housekeeper, while her father had worked.

A late developer, only in the past year at university had she felt her confidence grow in leaps and bounds. She'd been delighted to discover that being tall was no deterrent to making friends of both sexes, and she had even dated a few boys.

But never had she felt anything like the stomach-flipping, spine-tingling excitement Max Quintano's teasing smile and playful touch aroused in her.

A dreamy smile curved her wide mouth as she walked back up the beach and sat down on her towel, her besotted gaze focusing on his dark head, which was now a distant dot in the water. She could still feel the imprint of his arms as he had lifted her, the touch of his fingers against her breast on her heated skin.... Was this love or just fascination? she mused, unable to take her eyes off him.

Max turned in the water and struck back towards the shore, his tumescent flesh finally quietened by his strenuous swim. He had not had a woman since returning to Italy from Australia at the news of Paulo's death. He had endured four months of celibacy and was certain that this was the reason for his extreme reaction to the lovely Sophie.

Holding her in his arms, he had known she wanted him to kiss her—and he had certainly been aching to taste her lips and a lot more. But he had done the right thing and had left her alone, as Alex had requested. Alex was right. She was too young.

Feeling quite self-righteous, Max strode out of the water and flicked the hair from his eyes. He could see that she was still there on the beach, and as he approached she sat up and smiled. All his good intentions vanished. He was going to be in Sicily for a while, so what was wrong with a little flirtation with a beautiful girl?

'Come on, Sophie.' He reached a hand out to her. 'You have had too much sun. I'll walk you back to the hotel.' As she rose to her feet Max pressed a swift, soft kiss on the curve of her cheek. He heard the sharp intake of her breath, saw the sudden darkening of her incredible eyes his kiss had provoked, and before he made a complete fool of himself added, 'I'll show you the secret of the maze.'

As one week slipped into two Sophie didn't know if she was on her head or her heels. She was hopelessly in love for the first time in her life. Just the sight of Max Quintano set her heart aflutter, and when he spoke to her she was breathless. He treated her with a teasing friendliness, but his casual invitations to join him for a swim or a walk when she was off duty were enough to send her into seventh heaven. Of course she agreed like an eager puppy, and though they were not really dates they were both an agony and an ecstasy to her foolish heart. Max was the perfect gentleman at all times, and as much as Sophie wanted him to he never progressed past a kiss on her cheek.

Two weeks after first meeting Max, Sophie walked out of her bedroom and into the sitting room of the chalet she shared with her friend Marnie, the head receptionist of the hotel. Sophie was sure that tonight would be the night all her dreams would be fulfilled. Max had asked her out to dinner at a restaurant in Palermo—at last, a proper date!

'So what do you think, Marnie?' Sophie asked as she made a quick twirl. She had bought the sophisticated green silk designer gown from the hotel boutique that afternoon, hoping to impress Max.

'Let me guess—you are meeting Max Quintano?' Marnie quipped.

'Yes.' Sophie beamed. 'But do I look okay?'

'You look stunning! Max will be knocked for six. But are you sure you know what you are doing?' Marnie asked with a frown. 'I've warned you before about Max and his women. I even showed you a magazine article, remember? I can understand how you feel, but he is a lot older than you, and a sophisticated, experienced man. You're young, with your education to complete. Don't throw it all away on a brief affair—because that is all it can ever be.'

Sophie stiffened. 'I know, and I've heard all the rumours, but I'm sure those stories are vastly exaggerated.'

'Believe what you like—teenagers usually do,' Marnie said dryly. 'All I am saying is be careful. Max is a multi-millionaire with a matching lifestyle. He rarely stays here for more than the odd weekend. The only reason he is here now is to fill in for his father and his family after the death of his brother. But that is about to change, because I heard today the rest of the family are coming soon—and when they do, Max will not hang around for long.'

'You don't know that for sure,' Sophie said, her heart plummeting in her breast at the thought of Max leaving.

'No, I don't. But Max and his father do not have the closest relationship in the world. I understand that although he gets on well with his extended family, the person he cares the most about is his stepsister, Gina. It's well known that they have had an on-off relationship for years. Some say she tolerates his other women because she is dedicated to her career as a doctor and not interested in marriage. But rumour has it that Old Man Quintano told Max ages ago he would not countenance such a relationship. As far as he is concerned they are brother and sister, and anything else between them is unthinkable. But circumstances change, and Max is very much his own master, and if and when he does decide to marry I wouldn't be surprised if Gina was his bride. So be warned, Sophie, and don't do anything foolish.'

Sophie was saved from responding by the ringing of the doorbell, but her happiness of five minutes ago had vanished. However, it returned the moment she opened the door and saw Max, starkly handsome and elegantly clad in an immaculately tailored suit. His tall figure oozed sex appeal, and Sophie's already pounding heart leapt in her breast.

Max turned a smiling face towards the open door and looked at Sophie. For a moment he was struck dumb. Her mass of blond hair was swept up in an intricate knot on top of her head. Her exquisite face was delicately made up to enhance her superb bone structure and fabulous green eyes. As for what she was wearing—the mid-thigh-length sheath of emerald-green silk outlined every feminine curve and lay straight across her high firm breasts. Damn it, he was getting aroused just looking at her.

'You look amazing—and remarkably you're ready,' he said, thinking that she wasn't the only one—he could have quite happily ravished her there and then.

'Yes.'

She smiled at him and the breath left his body. Max had to remind himself once again that he had promised Alex he wouldn't seduce her—but the trouble was, Sophie intrigued him on every level. She made him laugh, she was clever beyond her years and she was a great companion. As for her physical appearance—he only had to look at her to want her. He should never have asked her out tonight, he realised, because he did not trust himself to keep his hands off her.

Sophie sensed none of Max's doubts, either during the short car ride or as he took her arm and led her into the restaurant—she was simply too excited.

Max ordered champagne, and when their glasses were filled he raised his and said, 'To a beautiful girl and a beautiful night.'

Sophie's face heated at his mention of night. Did he mean what she hoped he meant? Was he at last going to move their relationship to the next level? Kiss her and then make love to her? Yes, she decided as his deep, dark eyes smiled into hers and they touched glasses. With that simple exchange, the mood had been set for the evening.

Sophie let Max order for her, and as course followed course and the champagne flowed freely she fell ever deeper under his spell. They talked about everything and nothing, and Max punctuated their conversation with a smile or the touch of his hand on hers. He fed her morsels of food she had never tried before, watching her every reaction with amusement and something more. By the end of the meal Sophie knew she was totally in love with Max.

'That was a perfect meal.' She sighed happily as Max paid the bill.

Perfect food, maybe, Max thought. But pure torture for him. He was white-knuckled with the strain of keeping his hands off her. He must have been mad to think he could have just a mild flirtation with Sophie, and when he slipped an arm around her waist and led her out of the crowded restaurant it was nearly his undoing. She was tall, and when she leant into his side they were a perfect fit, her hip moving sexily against his thigh.

'I am so glad you brought me here.' She turned her head to smile up into his face. Her teeth were even and brilliant white against the light golden tan of her skin and he felt his body tighten another notch.

He was no masochist. This had to stop or he was in real danger of losing control—not something he ever did. Dropping his arm from her waist, Max opened the car door for her—but it did not stop his heart hammering in his chest. She looked so utterly exquisite and so damn naïve she hadn't the sense to hide her feelings.

'My pleasure,' he said, and abruptly slammed the door.

By the time he slid behind the wheel and started the car he had his body under control. As he manoeuvred the vehicle along the winding road back to the hotel he glanced at Sophie and realised he had no right to be angry with her. It wasn't her fault she had the looks and the body of a temptress and stopped men in their tracks, he thought dryly as he brought the car to a halt outside her chalet.

After their laughter and intimacy over the dinner table Sophie sensed Max's mood had inexplicably changed, and when the engine stopped she glanced up at him and wondered what she had done wrong.

'Home again,' she said inanely, and blushed as she realised she was way out of his league in the sophistication stakes. But in the next moment he proved her wrong.

'Ah, Sophie,' he drawled huskily. 'What am I going to do with you?'

She saw the sensual smile that curved his firm lips as he reached to slide his arm around her waist and pull her close to the hard wall of his chest. He growled something softly, something she did not understand, and then his mouth covered hers and she didn't care.

It was as though a starburst exploded in her brain, sending shock waves to every nerve-ending in her body. He slid his tongue seductively between her softly parted lips, exploring the sweet, moist interior, and her hands involuntarily reached up to clasp around his neck. His kiss was more than she could ever have imagined, and Sophie closed her eyes and gave herself up to the wonder of his embrace. She felt his hand stroke up to cup her breast, and as his thumb grazed the silk-covered, suddenly taut peak, a fiery wave of desire scorched through her veins.

'*Dio!* How I want you,' Max groaned.

Sophie's fingers were tangled in the sleek dark hair of

his head, and her tongue—at first tentatively and then te-
naciously—duelled with his as an ever-increasing hunger
consumed her.

Max heard her moan when he finally lifted his head,
and saw the passion in her dazzling green eyes. He knew
she was his for the taking. He almost succumbed—after
all, he was not made of stone, and denying his body was
not something he was used to. But he had made a promise
to Alex, so he had to rein in his carnal impulses.

Gently he pushed her back against the seat, and got out
of the car, drawing in a few deep, steadying breaths as he
walked around to open her door. 'Come on, *cara.*'

Hazy-eyed, Sophie glanced at the hand Max held out.
It took an enormous effort on her part to still the shaking
in her own hand and take the help he was offering, and step
out of the car.

She looked at the staff chalet and back at Max, her
body still strumming with excitement, not sure what to
do, what to say.

Sensing her uncertainty, Max curved an arm around her
waist and led her to the door. Once there, he turned her in
his arms and narrowed his dark eyes on her bemused
face—he would make it easy for her.

'Thank you for a lovely evening, Sophie. I won't come
in. I have some international calls to make—different time
zones, you understand.' He brushed his lips against her
brow and said regretfully, 'I am leaving tomorrow, but
maybe we will dine out again the next time I am here?'

Max wanted her, but he had a growing suspicion that
once with Sophie would never be enough. He didn't
believe in love, but he was astute enough to recognise

that what he felt for Sophie and how he lost control around her could very easily become dangerous to his peace of mind.

'Thank you—I would like that,' she murmured.

Max saw the naked adoration and the hurt in her eyes, and much as he wanted Sophie he knew Alex was right—she wasn't for him. He had watched her with the guests, the staff and with the children she quite happily looked after whenever she was asked. She was so caring and everyone adored her. Sophie deserved the very best, and he was far too much of a cynic to believe in love and happy ever after—whilst she was too young and too much of a romantic for the kind of affair he enjoyed. The timing wasn't right. Maybe in a few years, when she had completed her studies, and if she was still single…who knew…?

'Good night, sweet Sophie.' Because he couldn't resist touching her one last time, he lifted a finger and traced the outline of her lips, saw her smile. 'That's better. A young girl like you should always be smiling,' he drawled softly, his dark eyes enigmatic on her beautiful face.

He opened the chalet door, and with a hand at her back urged her inside with a wry twist of his lips. She was temptation on legs, and far too responsive and eager for her own good—not every man had his self-control.

'And be careful,' Max warned her as frustration rose up in him. He spun on his heel and left. His decision was made. He would take a flying visit to Russia, to iron out a few problems with the manager of his Russian operation. As he recalled, the company's receptionist, Nikita, was a very inventive lover. With the arrogant confidence of a wealthy man in his prime, he told himself the world was full of beautiful women more than willing to share his bed. He didn't need Sophie, and he would dismiss her from his mind.

Sophie watched Max walk away, wishing he would at least look back and give her some sign that he cared. But it was in vain.

Later that night, when Marnie found her curled up on the sofa, red-eyed from weeping and looking miserable, she gave Sophie the benefit of her opinion.

'What did you expect after one dinner date? An avowal of love? Cheer up, girl. Max Quintano can have any woman he wants and he knows it. You were a pleasant diversion while he was here.' She shrugged. 'Who knows? If he returns he might take you out again, and if he does just remember what I told you before: a brief affair is the best any woman can hope for from him.'

Marnie's words didn't help, but at least they made Sophie face up to reality. Her first ever crush on a man and it had to be on Max Quintano—a much older, super-rich mining tycoon, and a womaniser by all accounts. Where had her brain been? He was as far out of her reach as the moon. Her mistake had been in mistaking a teenage crush for true love, she told herself flatly, and she had to get over it. At least she hadn't slept with him….

But somehow that thought gave her no comfort at all.

CHAPTER TWO

Seven years later

ON SATURDAY afternoon Sophie parked her ancient car on the drive and, taking her suitcase from the back she breathed a sigh of relief as she entered her old home. Timothy, her brother, ran down the hall to meet her and, dropping her suitcase, she swept him up in her arms and kissed him.

'Hello, darling,' she said as she carried him into the elegant living room to find his mother and their father.

Sophie looked at her stepmother, Margot, and then at her father. Immediately she sensed the tension in the atmosphere and wondered what was wrong.

'Oh, good you have arrived,' Margot said.

No, *Hello—how are you*? Sophie thought dryly, and sat down on the sofa, still holding Tim.

'I suppose we should be honoured you can spare the time to visit your brother with your jet-setting lifestyle. Where is it this time?'

'Venice, for a three-day international conference on global resources. But I don't have to leave until tomorrow night, so I have more than enough time to babysit this little man.' Sophie hugged Timothy closer on her knee and added, 'Why don't you and Dad make a night of it and stay at the hotel until tomorrow? I don't mind.' That should put a smile on Margot's face, she thought.

Two hours later Sophie was sitting in the stainless steel kitchen of the house she had been born in, feeding Tim his favourite tea of fish fingers and mulling over how her life had changed.

Five years ago, when she had graduated from university, Sophie had taken a year off to go backpacking around the world. On her return she had discovered that her father's new secretary was also his pregnant girlfriend. Marriage had followed, and Meg the housekeeper had departed at Margot's request—much to Sophie's disgust. And four months later her adorable young brother had arrived.

Sophie had been besotted with Tim ever since, and if she was honest he was the main reason she tended to go along with whatever Margot wanted. He was why she had agreed to Margot's last-minute request for a babysitter so they could attend a glamorous charity ball at a top London hotel.

Sophie glanced around the ultra-modern kitchen. The family home in Surrey had been totally renovated by Margot, and she barely recognised the interior any more. But at least, with the help of a small legacy from her mother, Sophie had her own apartment, overlooking the sea in Hove. The commute into London was not something she would like to do every day, but then she didn't have to. She was a brilliant linguist, and her work as a freelance translator took her all over the world. She had built up an impressive list of corporate and private clients.

She had spent the last eight weeks with a trade delegation, travelling around China, and before that six weeks working in South America. This weekend was the first time she had been home in months. It wasn't that she disliked Margot—after all, she was only two years older than Sophie—in fact they should have had a lot in common, but unfortunately they didn't. Margot was a social animal who loved the high life—the best restaurants and the right places to go and see and be seen. But to give her her due Margot, for all her love of society and designer clothes, was a good mother and would not leave Tim with anyone she didn't know.

Much as she loved her brother, it was with a sense of relief that Sophie left the next afternoon to catch her flight to Venice. She wasn't imagining it—the atmosphere between her dad and Margot really had been no better when they'd returned at lunchtime than it had when they'd left the evening before. Something was not right in their relationship. But as long as it didn't affect Tim, she wasn't going to worry.

She had enough to worry about going to Italy again for the first time in seven years. The very thought brought back a host of unwanted memories of her one and only love affair—and of what a complete and utter idiot she had been. She had fallen for Max Quintano like a ton of bricks, and when he had left the hotel in Sicily where she worked, she had been hurt. But when he had returned a week later she had fallen into his bed without a moment's hesitation. After he had taken her innocence she had leapt at his proposal of marriage, and had even agreed to keep it a secret until he could meet her father.

For all of two days she had been deliriously happy—that was until she had discovered the kind of open marriage he had in mind....

A cynical smile twisted her lush lips. Still, she had learnt a valuable lesson from the experience—men were not to be trusted. That lesson had been reinforced over the years as she'd seen how a lot of them behaved as soon as they arrived at a conference well away from wife and family. Sophie had lost count of the number of times married men had hit on her, and she had developed an icy stare and a cool put-down to perfection.

The following Tuesday evening Sophie walked into the ballroom of a top Venetian hotel on the arm of Abe Asamov. Abe was a fifty-something, barrel-chested and bald-headed Russian who barely reached her shoulder. She had been delighted to see him arrive at the hotel this morning, for the second day of the conference, because his was a friendly face amongst a sea of strangers.

Abe was witty, and took great delight in fostering a ruthless reputation. Only Sophie knew he was devoted to his wife and family. In her last year at university she had spent her summer vacation in Russia, teaching his four grandchildren English.

When Abe had asked her to be his partner at this gala dinner-dance, she had agreed. The company she was temporarily contracted to had been overjoyed, because Abe Asamov was a billionaire oilman and owned a great deal of Russia's resources. Sophie wasn't sure she believed Abe's claim that he spoke only Russian, but she didn't care because she was glad of his company.

'You realise, Sophie, that they will all think you are my lady-friend.' Abe said in his native Russian, grinning up at her as the waiter showed them to their table. 'No ordinary man could look at a beautiful blonde like you and imagine you have a brain.' He chuckled. 'I think I will enjoy fooling people tonight.'

'Watch it, Abe.' She grinned, knowing he was no threat to her. 'Remember you are a married man—and if that was meant to be a compliment it was a bit of a backhanded one.'

'You sound just like my wife.' Abe grinned back, and they both laughed as they took their seats.

Seated comfortably and with a glass of champagne in her hand, Sophie glanced around the room, taking in the other guests there that evening. Many she knew through her work. There was the ambassador, Peter, and his wife Helen, and next to them a couple who worked for the Italian government—Aldo and his wife Tina. There were also two Spanish men—Felipe and Cesare—whom Sophie was seated next to. Very pleasant company, she decided, and, taking a sip of her drink, she began to relax and look at her surroundings.

The dinner tables were set around a small dance floor, and at one end on a raised dais a jazz band played background music. The evening was a glittering showcase of the powerful elite of Europe. The men looked immaculate in dinner suits, and the women were dressed in designer gowns and jewels worth millions. But Sophie did not feel intimidated. Over the years she had worked and mingled with some of the richest people from all around the world—even crowned heads of countries. As a result, she had acquired the social skills and sophistication needed in such company.

At home, jeans and a sweater were her favoured form of dress, but she had amassed what she called her 'business wardrobe'. The black satin Dior gown she wore tonight was one of her favourites, as were the crystal necklace and earrings. She knew she looked good and could hold her own in any crowd.

Feeling relaxed, Sophie glanced across the dance floor as a group of late arrivals took their seats and her green eyes widened in appalled recognition…Max Quintano and his stepsister Gina. Her shocked gaze skimmed over his hard, handsome profile and moved swiftly away. She was almost sure he hadn't seen her.

With her heart pounding, Sophie manoeuvred her chair so she could turn her back slightly towards his table and hopefully remain unnoticed.

She turned to Cesare, seated on her left, and asked in Spanish, 'So, what do you do?' On hearing his response she focused all her attention on him. 'An earth scientist? How interesting.'

Fool that she was, Sophie could not believe she hadn't made the connection between global resources and Max Quintano before now.

Across the other side of the room Max Quintano smiled at something Gina said, not having registered a word. He had recognised Sophie Rutherford the minute he had entered the room. Her blond head was unmistakable, with the fabulous hair swept up in an elegant pleat, revealing her long neck and the perfect set of her bare shoulders. The cut of her gown displayed the silken smoothness of her back and the slight indentation of her spine. A spine he had once trailed kisses down. His body tightened at the memory.

He saw the exact moment when she recognised him, and watched as the cold-hearted bitch turned away in fright. He had despised her with a depth of passion he had not known he was capable off when they had parted, and the way he had dealt with it had been to ruthlessly blot her out of his mind for many years. Then, on the death of his father four months ago, due to a massive heart attack, the name of Rutherford had reared its ugly head again in the shape of Nigel Rutherford. Surprisingly, two months later on a brief trip to South America, Sophie Rutherford had been the object of much speculation. Twice in as many months he had been confronted with the very name he had tried to forget.

As executor of his father's estate, and with his stepmother distraught at her husband's death and in no fit state to concentrate on the running of Quintano Hotels, naturally Max had stepped in to help. An audit of the family's business had disclosed that it was running at a very healthy profit, but there were one or two bad debts outstanding. The largest one was the Elite Agency, London—Nigel Rutherford's firm. Max had soon discovered that they were not just slow at paying their clients' accommodation bills, they had not paid at all for almost a year.

How it had been overlooked Max could only surmise. Maybe his father had been in failing health for some time without believing it. He could relate to that feeling, because he had done the same thing seven years ago. When Max had been told he might have cancer he hadn't wanted to believe it, and a couple of nights in the lovely Sophie's bed had fed his illusion of invincibility. How wrong he had been…. So he could not blame his father for doing the same.

On further investigation into the bad debt he had discovered that Quintano Hotels was not the only firm owed massive amounts of money by Nigel Rutherford. Max had joined with the rest in calling for a creditors' meeting, which was to be held next Monday in London. However, Max had no intention of going—he was leaving it to the lawyers and accountants to take care of. He could not care less if the Elite Agency went under, along with its owner, as long as Quintano Hotels got paid.

But now, with the beautiful but shallow daughter only thirty feet away, sipping a glass of champagne and smiling as if she hadn't a care in the world, a different scenario sprang to mind. If *he* attended the meeting in London he knew he would have no trouble convincing the other creditors to bankrupt her father's firm; he was a very persuasive man.

Sophie was occupied at the moment, but next week he would make it plain to Nigel Rutherford that he wanted to meet his daughter *again*! He had already waited years, so a week or two longer wouldn't matter. With ruthless cynicism Max decided it would be interesting to watch Sophie squirm when she realised who was responsible for her father's downfall, and very satisfying to see how far she would go to save him.

Sophie Rutherford was the only woman who had ever walked out on him, and it had taken him a long time to get over the insult. Now fate had once again put her back in his life—and in his power, if he wanted to use it. With his body hardening at the mere sight of her he knew he did, and the iniquitous plan took root in his mind.

* * *

It had been an appalling trick of fate that had sent Max dashing back to Sicily and Sophie seven years ago. He had returned from five days in Russia to his apartment in Rome still celibate, and still resolved to stay away from Sophie. He had called an old girlfriend and arranged to have dinner that night, and also arranged to have lunch with Gina the following day—Friday.

His date had not been a success, and he had gone to his office early the next morning and finally caught up with the personal items of mail his PA had not opened. A casual glance at the report from the medical he had taken a couple of weeks earlier had told him there was a query about one of his results and that he would need to contact a Dr Foscari.

Two hours later Max had been sitting numb with shock as Dr Foscari informed him that his urine test had revealed irregularities in his testosterone levels—a sign of testicular cancer. The doctor had gone on to explain that it was the most prevalent form of cancer in males between the ages of twenty and forty-four, but was easily treated. He'd told Max not to worry, because the test wasn't certain, but as a precaution he had made an appointment with a top consultant at the best hospital in Rome for the following week.

Max had walked out of the clinic with fear clawing at his gut. But he had been furious at the mere suggestion he could be ill, and had determined to seek a second opinion. Gina was an oncologist; she would know the leading specialist in the field. He would talk to her over lunch, tell her his fears, knowing she would keep his confidence.

By the time lunch had been over Max had known more

than he'd ever wanted to know about his suspected illness. Gina, in her forthright manner, had immediately called Dr Foscari, and after speaking to him had told Max not to panic. She had explained that there might be other causes for the irregular testosterone levels, and that anyway there was now a ninety-five per cent success rate in the treatment of testicular cancer. At Max's insistence she had gone on to outline the worst-case scenario if it *was* cancer. She had asked him if he had noticed any little lumps, if he was feeling unusually tired or suffering any loss of libido—all of which he had vehemently denied.

When she had then begun to explain in detail the treatment and the side effects—the possible loss of virility, the freezing of sperm as a precaution against infertility—Max had actually felt sick. To reassure him, Gina had offered to contact a colleague at a clinic in America who was a renowned specialist in the field, in case a second opinion was needed.

He had suggested flying straight to America, but she had told him not to be so impulsive and added that as nothing was going to happen in the next few days he should try to have a relaxing weekend.

Max hadn't been able to ignore Gina's opinion because he trusted her completely. He had done since their parents had married, when he was four and she was five, and they had instantly become as close as biological siblings, with a genuine liking for each other that had lasted into adulthood. She had supported him in his ambition to be a geologist, and he had done the same for her in her medical ambition and in her personal life.

'Max? Max!'

The sound of his name intruded on unpleasant memories of the past. He looked across the table at Gina, and the other two people in their party—Rosa and her husband Ted.

Gina and Rosa were lovers, and had been for years. Ted had his own reasons for keeping the secret—Rosa was the mother of his two children, and Max knew he had a long-term mistress. As for Max, he kept the secret because Gina wanted him to. She was convinced that their parents would be horrified if they knew the truth, and that the potential scandal of the relationship might harm her career prospects.

'Sorry, Gina.' He smiled. Personally, he thought Gina was wrong, and believed that not many people were bothered about a person's sexual preference in the twenty-first century, but it wasn't his secret to reveal.

'You have seen her? Sophie Rutherford?' Gina prompted. 'Are you okay?'

'Yes, fine.' He saw the concern in her eyes and added, 'I can't say I am impressed by her choice of partner.' He cast a glance at the blond-headed Venus in question, his mouth curling in a cynical smile. 'But I'm not surprised.'

Always a man of action, Max was not given to moods of reflection. But now, as he ate the food put before him, he found it hard to concentrate on the present when the woman responsible for so many painful memories of his past was seated just a few yards away. Seeing Sophie again had brought to mind in every vivid detail perhaps the worst episode in his life all those years ago….

Max had left Gina outside the restaurant, his mind in flux, and slowly walked back in the direction of his office.

For a self-confident man who prided himself on always being in control, a man who made business decisions involving millions on a daily basis and never doubted his course of action, it had been sobering to realise he was just as susceptible as the next man to the unfamiliar emotions of doubt and fear. He enjoyed his work, was very successful and very wealthy, and he had gone his own way for years with very little thought to the future. But now he'd been forced to face the fact he might not have one, and suddenly everything he had achieved didn't amount to much.

If he dropped dead tomorrow his family and a couple of friends might grieve for a while, but eventually it would be as though he'd never existed.

A few days before Max had thought he had all the time in the world, that marriage and children were something he wouldn't have to consider for years. He had thought in his arrogance that the *timing* had not been right for an *affair* with Sophie—that he didn't need her. But with the threat of serious illness hanging over him *time* had suddenly become vitally important.

Impulsively he had called his pilot, and an hour later had been flying back to Sicily—and Sophie. Alex be damned! He needed Sophie's uncomplicated company, her open adoration, her stunning body, and he wasn't going to wait. He was going to have her—and she might just be the last woman he had in this life.

Max had glanced around the familiar view of the hotel gardens. His dark eyes had narrowed on a group of three young boys in the swimming pool, playing water polo with a girl. The girl had been Sophie, and as he'd watched she had hauled herself out of the water and flopped down on a sunbed, the young boys sprawling on the ground around her.

The mere sight of her in the familiar pink bikini had knocked any lingering doubt from his brain and he'd felt his body stir and strode towards her.

'Hello, Sophie. Still playing around, I see,' he drawled mockingly, and tugged lightly on the long wet braid of her hair falling down her back.

Her head turned and her green eyes widened to their fullest extent. 'Max—you're back! I didn't know.' And the rush of colour and the welcoming smile on her face were all Max could have hoped for and more.

'Dare I ask if you are free for the evening?' Of course her answer would be yes. He never doubted it for a moment. And the events of the morning in Rome were pushed to the back of his mind as his dark gaze lingered over her scantily clad form. 'I thought a drive along the coast, and a picnic, perhaps?' He wondered why he had denied his own desire the day he met her, three weeks ago.

'I'd love it,' she said, a smile curving her luscious mouth, and he couldn't resist pulling her into his arms and kissing her.

Lifting his head, his brown eyes dark with need, he searched her lovely face. *Dio!* How he wanted this woman. There was certainly nothing wrong with his testosterone levels. In fact, if he didn't get away fast the rest of the guests around the pool would be well aware of that, too.

He sucked in a deep, steadying breath and gently pulled her away from him. 'I'll pick you up at eight.' And he turned and walked away.

Sophie watched Max's departure, her eyes drifting

lovingly over him, the misery and doubt of the last week forgotten in her euphoria at seeing Max again.

Later that evening Max helped her out of the car and, lifting a hamper from the back, he took her hand firmly in his.

'Where are we?' Sophie asked. He had stopped the car at the harbour of a small town, and she glanced around her with pleasure. Coloured lights danced in the darkness, following the curve of the harbour that had a dozen yachts bobbing in gently lapping water.

'La Porto Piccolo,' he said, looking down at her with a reminiscent smile on his starkly handsome face. 'It was a favourite haunt of my friend Franco and I when we were younger. We bought our first yacht together when we were nineteen and hoping to impress the girls. We have always kept it here, away from our families' prying eyes. It is small, but we had some great times.' Taking her hand, he helped her on board.

Sophie wasn't sure she liked the implication in his words. Was this some kind of love boat? And just how many girls had Max entertained on board? But then she spotted a table and two chairs set out on the polished wood deck. 'We are eating here?' she asked.

'Yes.' He placed the hamper on the table and drew her gently into his arms. 'It is a beautiful night, and I thought you would appreciate dining on the deck.' He brushed his lips against her hair. 'You have no idea how much I want to please you, in every way.' His lips lowered to brush gently against her mouth and she was stunned by the gentleness in his gaze.

Max cared, he really cared for her, and involuntarily

Sophie raised her hand to rest on his broad chest. 'You already do,' she said with blunt honesty. 'I missed you so much when you were away. I missed your unruly black hair, your teasing smile…' She flicked a silken lock from his brow. 'I'm glad you are back.'

'You can show me how much later.' Max covered her hand on his chest with his own and bent his dark head so that his mouth lightly nuzzled her neck. Sophie shuddered when she felt the flick of his tongue against her sensitive skin. 'But first a tour of the yacht, and then food,' he prompted.

With his arm around her waist, his fingers splayed across the soft skin of her midriff, Sophie was too aware of the magic of his touch to notice the boat. She had a fleeting view of one small cabin, and heard Max's comment about 'two berths', and then he was opening a door into the only other cabin.

'Duck your head,' he instructed, ushering her inside and closing the door behind them. The cabin was tiny, and lit only by the lights of the harbour, which were casting flickering shadows on the double bunk that almost filled the space. 'It is only for sleeping,' he murmured, his breath warm against her brow.

Sophie had never felt less like sleeping. And when Max's hand tightened on her waist and turned her to face him all she felt was breathless. She looked up, every nerve-ending tingling at the close proximity of his great body, and stared as if mesmerised by his glittering dark eyes, any thought of caution vanished.

Then his mouth found hers, his tongue moving within it with a deeply erotic passion, and Sophie was lost to everything but the incredible sensations shooting through her body.

He lifted his head and looked searchingly down at her.

'You want this?' he prompted huskily, his voice barely audible as he gently brushed a strand of silken hair from her cheek.

'Yes,' she gasped, and in moments they were naked on the bed.

A long time later Sophie lay collapsed on top of him, breathless and shaking—she had never known such pleasure existed. Max gently lifted her chin with his index finger. 'You should have told me I was your first.'

'And my only,' she sighed. 'I love you so much.'

'Oh, Sophie, I adore you. You are truly priceless— don't ever change,' he drawled softly.

'I am changed now, thanks to you,' she whispered.

'I know.' Max kissed her swollen lips again—he couldn't help himself. 'But it is I who should be thanking you. You have given me something precious and worth much more than you can ever imagine.'

Never before had he made love to a virgin, and never before had he met with such a wild reciprocal passion. He had lost touch with everything but the incredible agonising pleasure he had felt as he came inside her.

But that was the problem. He had done just that— forgotten protection. He looked into her happy love-lit eyes, about to tell her, but couldn't bring himself to spoil the moment. Instead he heard himself say, 'Marry me.' And realised he meant it…. Whatever the future held, Sophie was to be his and his alone….

With anger simmering just below the surface, Max cast a hard, cold glance at the catalyst of his trip down memory lane. With the benefit of hindsight he realised his proposal had probably been a simple gut reaction to the massive blow his male ego had suffered at the thought of testicular cancer. But at the time, after having sex with her, he had deluded himself into believing it was something more and asked her to marry him.

Max glanced across at Sophie again, and this time his gaze lingered, his dark eyes narrowing as he saw her smiling and charming the men either side of her. He saw Abe Asamov stroke her cheek with one finger, and his mouth curled in a bitter, cynical smile—a smile that was strained to the limit as she got up to dance with the man. The easy familiarity between Sophie and Abe was unmistakable.

Dio! Sophie was certainly sleeping with him, and it could only be for one reason—money. Disgust churned his gut. When he saw them leave the dance floor, and watched her kiss the fat Russian on the cheek, he dismissed any notion of waiting a week or two to speak to her. In fact another minute was too long, and he changed his plan accordingly.

It was said that revenge was best taken cold, and Max told himself he felt nothing but ice-cold anger for the beautiful Sophie and what she had become. He rose to his feet and excused himself. He had once thought the timing wasn't right for an affair with Sophie, and then changed his mind. Two days later he had been dumped unceremoniously by the heartless witch. Now he had changed it back again, and this time he would be the one to walk away. But not until he had sated himself in her gorgeous body....

CHAPTER THREE

EVERY SELF-PROTECTIVE instinct Sophie possessed was telling her to turn and run. She'd known coming back to Italy was not a good idea, and seeing Max confirmed it. But she knew she had to get through this dinner—if only to prove that she was a true professional and Max Quintano meant nothing, in fact less than nothing, to her.

Luckily for Sophie, Abe had asked her to interpret Cesare's conversation and she readily agreed; if she kept her eyes on Cesare and Abe she could almost pretend that Max and Gina didn't exist.

Back at university, after her brief affair with Max, it had been hard—but with the help of her friends and by throwing herself into work she had finally got over him and convinced herself she didn't care. Now it was galling to have to admit that it still hurt to see Max with Gina.

For the next hour Sophie ate, drank and smiled in all the right places, but she was intensely conscious of Max Quintano's powerful presence. She felt as though his eyes were on her, and that made the hair on the back of her neck stand on end. It took every bit of will-power she had to chat normally and avoid glancing back at the hateful man. The realisation that just the sight of him could upset her so much after all this time gnawed away at her. To compensate she sparkled all the brighter with the clearly admiring Cesare, so much so that Abe picked up on her distress.

He raised a finger to her cheek and stroked her jawline. 'Sophie?' She looked into his shrewd blue eyes. 'You are trying too hard—whoever it is you are trying to avoid, my dear,' he murmured, 'use me, not young Cesare. You could hurt him. But I have broad shoulders, and I don't mind playing the game.'

'You see too much,' Sophie sighed, and when Abe asked her to dance she managed an almost natural smile and rose to her feet, going gracefully into his arms.

Surprisingly, for all his bulk, Abe was a good dancer, and Sophie relaxed into the music, her tall, graceful body drawing the eye of many appreciative males—and one in particular.

'You're a very beautiful woman, as I've told you before,' Abe said as the music ended and with a guiding hand around her waist he led her back towards the table. 'Whoever he was, he was a fool, and he didn't deserve you in the first place. You are worth the best, and don't you forget it.'

She looked at Abe's hard face and realised that not only was he an extremely nice man, but also extremely astute—no wonder he was a billionaire oil mogul.

'You're right.' She smiled and kissed his cheek. 'Thank you.' Why was she wasting her time getting upset all because she had had one disastrous love affair with a womanising bastard? It was time she moved on with her life, she thought determinedly.

'Excuse me,' a deep, dark voice drawled mockingly,

and Max Quintano appeared in front of them. 'May I claim your partner for the next dance?'

Abe looked up at Max, not in the least intimidated by his great height, and slowly let his eyes inspect the man, before quirking an enquiring brow at Sophie and demanding in his own language to know what had been said. She was too shocked by Max's sudden interruption and request to think of lying, and she told Abe.

'Ah.' He looked back at Max. 'You want my woman?' he managed in English, and his blue eyes danced with a wicked light.

Sophie knew Abe was enjoying himself, and she glanced up at Max through the thick veil of her lashes. The look of cynical contempt on his harshly handsome face infuriated her. Abe had implied that she was his lover, and it was obvious Max believed him. He had a nerve to sneer at her, when *he* was the one with a legion of lovers and his long-term lover sitting at the other side of the dance floor. So why was he insisting on dancing with her given his obvious distain?

'I hope you will allow me the pleasure of dancing with your charming companion. Sophie and I are old friends.' His dark eyes narrowed challengingly on Abe.

Abe let go of her waist and threw up his hands in a theatrical gesture. 'I am not her keeper—ask her.' Abe suddenly seemed to know a lot more English than anyone had given him credit for—Sophie included.

Max's dark head turned and his gaze captured hers. 'May I have this dance, Sophie? Your partner does not seem to mind,' he opined, with a sardonic curl of his firm lips.

'Max—what a surprise,' she said coldly. Words couldn't begin to describe the anger that had swelled up inside her as the two men talked over her as if she wasn't there. 'I didn't know you could dance. Did Gina teach you?' she asked pointedly. The two-timing toad had the nerve to take a dig at her in front of everyone, and still demand that she dance with him.

'As a matter of fact she did. Amongst other things,' he said, grinning.

Shock kept her silent for a moment, his brazen reply adding insult to injury. Then, realising that standing in silence, sandwiched between two men on the edge of the dance floor, was arousing the antennae of the company around them, she said sweetly 'I'm sure she did. And, given she is your companion for the evening, shouldn't you be dancing with her?'

'No, Gina has other things on her mind,' he replied with an amused glance across at his table.

His callous indifference amazed her, and she allowed her gaze to rake angrily over him. He hadn't changed much. His black hair was cut shorter, and liberally sprinkled with grey, and the lines bracketing his mouth were slightly more pronounced. There was a hard edge about him, which was in direct contrast to the laughing, teasing man she had known, but he was still strikingly attractive.

'I'm surprised you want to dance with me,' she finally said bluntly.

Max moved closer and held out his hand. 'You shouldn't be, Sophie. After all, we were once *extremely* close friends.' His glittering eyes mocked her, and for a moment she hesitated. But she didn't trust him not to blurt out something even more compromising if she refused, and the gossip it would cause was not something she wanted.

'I'd be delighted to dance with you, Mr Quintano,' she said with a coldly polite social smile, and put her hand in his.

Max sensed she hated the idea but was too polite to say so, and he deliberately linked his fingers through hers and felt the slight tremble in her hand. 'Now, that wasn't so hard,' he said, dipping his dark head to murmur in her ear as he led her onto the dance floor. He had won the first battle without her putting up much of a fight

As he stopped, he caught her other hand and deliberately held her at arm's length. 'You are looking well.' He allowed his dark gaze to sweep insolently over her. She was. Sophie Rutherford had turned into an exquisitely elegant lady—even if she did have the morals of an alley cat. 'More beautiful than ever, in fact. But I've been watching you, and some things never change. You are still as eager as ever where men are concerned—and Abe Asamov is quite some catch! You do realise he is a married man?' Max prompted cynically, and did what he had been aching to do since he'd first set eyes on her tonight. He pulled her close against his hard body and guided her expertly around the floor to the slow music.

The brush of his long legs against hers, the familiar warmth and scent of him, sent a tremor of what Sophie hoped was revulsion down her spine. His callous reference to her pathetic eagerness with him so long ago was making her squirm inside at how naïve she had been. A lamb led to the slaughter sprang to mind... But she didn't let it show. That girl was long gone. She was now a confident, sophisticated woman who could hold her own in any situation.

'So?' she said, with a casual shrug of one shoulder, even whilst tensing against the inevitable close body contact. 'I'm not looking for a husband.'

'No,' Max drawled, glancing down at her with hooded eyes. 'I more than most should know that you want wealth and pleasure. But the stress and strain of marriage, of caring for a husband—' he gave a wry grimace '—is certainly not for you.'

'You know me so well,' she said sweetly, and felt his strong hand stroke up her naked back and press her closer, until she was in contact with his broad chest. Much to her dismay, she was helpless to control the sudden tightening of her nipples, or the leap in her pulse-rate.

'You've got that right.' He slanted a glance down at the soft curve of her breasts revealed by the low-cut neckline and a sardonic smile twisted his firm lips. 'And I wouldn't mind getting to know you all over again. What do you say, Sophie?' he queried arrogantly. 'Me instead of the ape Abe? You know we were good together, and they do say a woman never forgets her first lover.'

With a supreme effort she hid her shock at his statement. Max was certainly direct, if not downright crude, and it seemed impossible to her now that she had ever thought she loved this man.

'You're disgusting,' she finally said bluntly, attempting to lean back from him. Being so close to him was playing havoc with her nervous system. Age hadn't dimmed his powerful animal magnetism, and even though she despised him she was drawn to him like a moth to a flame. She felt exactly the same as the first time she had set eyes on him, and she hated the powerless feeling he ignited in her.

'Maybe.' She felt his lips brush against the top of her head. 'But you haven't answered my question.'

'It isn't deserving of an answer.' She looked up into his hard face, her green eyes turbulent with the mixed emotions of fear and anger—at her own weakness almost as much as with him. 'I don't know why you even asked me to dance, given when we parted you never wanted to set eyes on me again. Or why I allowed good manners to influence me to agree, because *you* certainly have none.'

That Max thought she was capable of having an affair with Abe was bad enough, but that he actually had the nerve to suggest she swap lovers! 'I have not seen you in seven years, and if I don't see you again in seven times seven years it would still be too soon.'

'My, Sophie, what a shrew you have turned into—and here I was, trying to be kind,' he said silkily. 'I may not be quite as wealthy as Abe, but I can certainly keep you in the manner to which you have become accustomed. The gown is Dior, but your lover has short-changed you. As my mistress you would be wearing diamonds, not crystal, I promise you,' he ended mockingly.

'Why, you…' Words failed her. She didn't have to put up with this, she wasn't a star-struck nineteen-year-old any more, even if her traitorous body was still excited by the man. That he should endow her with his own despicable morality was the last straw, and she attempted to wriggle out of his grasp.

'Stop it,' Max warned, and his hand moved up her back

to hold her firmly against him, his long fingers splayed just below her shoulder blades. 'For your sake more than mine, I would prefer us to reach a mutual beneficial agreement without the avid interest of this crowd.'

'Agreement! What the hell are you talking about?' she demanded, beginning to feel like Alice in Wonderland when she fell down the rabbit hole…. No, more like the Mad Hatter, she amended.

When the music thankfully stopped, Sophie placed her hands on his chest to push him away, but his other arm tightened about her and she was unable to move.

She looked bitterly up at him, saw the flare of raw anger that hardened his eyes and watched his dark head lower. He wouldn't dare kiss her in public, she thought— just before his mouth brushed over hers in a brief, hard kiss. She was too surprised to resist, and her hard-won icy control shattered into a million pieces as the awareness she had been trying to deny from the moment she saw him again heated her blood and coloured her face.

When he lifted his head her hands were resting on his chest. She didn't know how they had got there, but she was humiliatingly aware that to anyone watching it must look as if she had consented to his kiss. 'God! You have no scruples at all, you bastard.'

'Where you are concerned, no. And now maybe Abe will have got the message. You were mine before you were his, and you will be mine again.'

'Have you lost your mind?' Sophie asked, but with her head spinning from the dizzying effect of his kiss it was her own mind she was worried about. 'I wouldn't have you gift-wrapped with bells on.'

'Yes, you will.' He disentangled his arms and laid a hand on her waist. 'Your reaction told me all I needed to know,' he said as he led her back to her table, his head bent solicitously towards her as he continued talking. 'I have heard glowing reports about you from a friend of mine in South America. Apparently, your career has really taken off. It seems you are in great demand—and not just for your language skills,' he drawled sardonically.

'You've heard?' She was horrified to think Max Quintano might know some of the people she worked for, but suddenly she realised how blind she had been. Of course he moved in the same sphere as a lot of her clients—why wouldn't he?

'The Chilean ambassador's son—a fantastic polo player—was quite besotted with you. Apparently when you arrived at his last cup match he couldn't take his eyes off you, and as a result he fell off his horse and broke a leg. But needless to say you didn't rush to his side.'

Sophie remembered the incident, and the gossip it had caused—which had shocked her because she barely knew the man in question. But she shrugged off his comment with a terse, 'So what?'

'I also heard your father is married again and you have a little brother.'

'Yes,' she answered mechanically. It was taking all of her will-power simply to walk beside him, when all she really wanted to do was run and hide. Away from him— and the curious eyes that were watching them.

'If you value their security, you will meet me tomorrow for lunch to discuss it. I will call at your hotel at noon,' he commanded, as they reached the table.

'We have nothing to discuss,' she muttered, as he pulled out a chair for her to sit down. She looked up into his taut, cynical face and wondered why on earth he wanted to see her again when he had the doting Gina—and what it had to do with her family.

'Be there,' he said with a silky smile. 'And thank you for the dance. It was very illuminating.' But the smile never reached his eyes and she watched numbly as he turned and said, 'Thank you, Abe,' his narrowed eyes glittering with triumph as they met the older man's.

Abe took a long time to answer, his cool blue gaze holding Max's, and then he shook his bald head. 'I do not need the thanks,' he said dryly. 'You have my...' He turned to Sophie and asked for the word for sympathy. She told him and he repeated it. 'My sympathy.'

'What do you mean by offering Quintano your sympathy?' Sophie asked Abe as soon as Max had walked away. 'I thought you were my friend. I can't stand the man, and I'm certainly not having lunch with the arrogant devil.'

'The Ice Queen cracks.' Abe grinned. 'And if you don't know why I offered the man sympathy, then maybe I am wrong and all is not lost,' he answered cryptically. 'In which case Quintano does not need my sympathy and we shall continue the game.' He called the waiter and ordered more champagne, toasting Sophie and teasing her with, 'My wife will be delighted when I tell her the story. We have been waiting for this for a long time—you are far too lovely to be alone.'

Sophie denied she had *any* interest in Max Quintano, and tried her best to appear unaffected by her encounter with him, but it was an uphill struggle. She sipped the champagne and joined in the conversation, but her emotions were all over the place.

She felt angry with Max for intruding into her life again and deliberately humiliating her by kissing her in front of a crowd of people—but also angry at herself for letting him. He was still with Gina, and if he had been serious about propositioning her then he was also still a woman-iser and beneath contempt. But then she already knew that, and the only thing to do was to dismiss him from her mind. As for his demand that she should have lunch with him—in his dreams!

She drained her champagne, and when Abe suggested coffee she agreed. They left shortly after.

Max watched them leave, his dark eyes burning with an unholy light. Abe Asamov would never get another chance with Sophie, he decided with ruthless implacabil-ity. He had the power to make sure she was his again for as long as he wanted her delectable body, and he was going to use it.

CHAPTER FOUR

BACK AT THE HOTEL Sophie stripped off her clothes and headed for the bathroom. She washed, then removed her make-up, and after brushing and braiding her hair pulled on a cotton nightshirt and slipped into bed. She was weary beyond belief and, sighing, she closed her eyes and snuggled under the covers.

But sleep was elusive. She moved restlessly, turning onto her stomach and burying her face in the pillow, trying to block out the image of Max from her brain—but it was no good. Meeting him tonight had stirred up a host of memories that she had tried her damnedest to forget.

From the first day she had met Max she had been totally besotted with him, and when he'd left the hotel two weeks later, after their one and only dinner date, she had been devastated. But with Marnie's help she had almost convinced herself it was for the best. Max Quintano was streets ahead of her in every way. As a mega-rich mining tycoon he was too old, too worldly and too wealthy to be tempted by an innocent young student, and she had begun to recognise that she had been extremely foolish to imagine otherwise.

That was until he had returned unexpectedly a week later. All her doubts and reservations had vanished like smoke in the wind when he'd asked her out again.

Much later, when trying to account for what had happened next, Sophie would realise she had been set up and seduced by an expert. But when he'd taken her to his yacht—a boat he'd actually told her had been more or less bought for the purpose—she had made no complaint. When he'd led her to the cabin, stripped her naked and laid her on the bed she had made no protest. Naked before a man for the first time in her life, she should have been nervous—but with Max she hadn't been. And when he'd joined her and begun to kiss her face, her eyelids, the soft curve of her cheek, she had reached for him.

Sophie could see his smile in her mind's eye even now, all these years later. His heavy-lidded eyes molten with desire as he took her mouth in a deeply passionate, hungry kiss—then her breasts, her stomach, everything else, until she was moaning and writhing, her whole body shaking. She had never felt such pleasure, and he'd taken her into realms of sensuality she had never known existed.

When he had discovered she was a virgin he had stilled for a moment, then moved again slowly. With erotic caresses from his hands and mouth he had driven her ever wilder, and thrust even deeper, until they'd moved together in perfect rhythm. Finally, with more powerful strokes, he had filled her to the hilt and driven her over the edge into a delirious climax, and, crying out, had joined her.

Stifling a moan, Sophie squirmed in the bed. Whatever else Max was, there was no denying he was a magnificent, considerate lover. She doubted that any woman had ever had a more incredibly satisfying initiation into sex—one that had been topped off with a proposal of marriage. Delirious with happiness, she had accepted immediately, and agreed that their engagement would remain secret until he had spoken to their respective fathers.

Wryly, she conceded that at the time she would have accepted black was white if Max had said so. But her state of euphoria had lasted just one more night, and their final day was etched into her brain for all time....

Eyes closed, she could picture Max perfectly as he had walked out of the hotel dining room after lunch on the Sunday afternoon.

Casually elegant in pale chinos and a loose cotton shirt, Max had moved with a lazy grace to lean against the reception desk, where Sophie had been helping out for a few hours, his gleaming dark eyes holding hers and a sensual smile playing around his lips.

'I was hoping we could enjoy a siesta,' he said, his long, tanned fingers closing over hers on the desktop Even after two nights of Max's incredible lovemaking and their secret engagement she still reddened. 'No need to blush, Sophie.' He chuckled. 'It is what all engaged couples do—in fact it is a tradition here in Sicily. And you would not want to upset the locals,' he teased, tongue in cheek.

'You are insatiable, sir,' she teased back. 'And I am not off duty until four.'

He glanced at his wristwatch, and then his knowledgeable eyes met hers again, a wealth of tenderness in their depths. 'Two hours—I suppose I can wait that long, but it will be hard,' he said, with a tilt of one ebony brow and a wicked grin, and Sophie burst out laughing.

But Sophie's laughter faded as someone distracted him by calling his name. He spun around, and she watched in surprise as Max dashed to the small, gamine-looking woman with close-cropped black hair approaching the desk, swept her up in his arms and kissed her on both cheeks. A tirade of Italian followed for the next five minutes, interspersed with much hand waving, before Max turned to walk back to the desk with his arm firmly around the other woman.

'Sophie, I want you to meet my sister Gina,' he declared. 'She decided to make a surprise visit.' And, smiling down at the other woman, he said, 'This is my friend Sophie.'

Sophie smiled shyly at Gina and held out her hand to the woman who would be her future sister-in-law. 'Pleased to meet you.'

Gina acknowledged her with a bright smile. 'The pleasure is all mine. You're very lovely.' She shook her hand, then immediately turned back to Max. 'Staying true to form, I see. It would take a bulldozer to flatten you!' She laughed, and although Sophie didn't get the joke, she thought to herself that Gina seemed friendly enough.

'Sophie, be a dear and order a light lunch and coffee to be sent up to my suite. Gina hasn't eaten yet, and we have a lot to discuss. I'll catch you later.'

Sophie watched Max walk away and enter the elevator with his arm still around Gina—and without a second glance for her. Slightly disturbed by his offhand manner, she felt her happy mood sink a little as she rang through to inform the kitchen of Max's requirements. Only after she had replaced the receiver did Marnie's warning come back to haunt her.

Gina wasn't his sister but his *step*sister—and the woman it was rumoured that Max had been having an affair with for years. Suddenly Sophie's shining confidence in her lover, her *fiancé*, took a nasty knock.

It didn't help when Marnie came in at four to take over from her. When she told her that Gina had arrived unexpectedly, the sudden pity in her friend's dark eyes simply increased Sophie's doubts. Feeling dejected and suspicious, she returned to the staff chalet and stripped off her uniform and took a shower. Grasping a big fluffy towel, she dried her body—and grimaced at the telltale stain.

Maybe it was the time of the month that was making her feel jealous and moody, she thought as she walked back into the bedroom and dressed casually in Capri pants and tee shirt. It also meant no lovemaking for a few days, which lowered her mood still further.

Too restless to settle, she prowled around the chalet, her eyes constantly drawn back to the telephone. Surely Max would ring soon, stepsister or no stepsister. He knew she was off duty at four.

When it got to five she could not stand to be cooped up inside any longer, so she decided to go for a walk around the gardens to the maze where Max had taken her the first day they met.

Sophie rolled over onto her back and squeezed her eyes tight to hold back the tears that threatened, even now, after all these years. She could hear their voices as clear as if it had been yesterday.

'Max, you have to tell the girl, if you really do intend

to marry her. Young women are much worldlier nowadays; she might handle the situation without so much as batting an eyelid.' Sophie recognised Gina's voice, and the urgency in it, and slowed her pace a little.

'Do you think so? I'm not so sure. She is very young, and not very worldly at all—unlike most women I know.'

What situation? Sophie wondered, all her earlier feelings of jealousy and doubt flooding back as she walked slowly towards the end of the hedge—and, if she had but known, towards the end of her dreams…

'In that case, why are you even contemplating marrying her?'

'Because, among other things, I was careless and didn't use any protection. She could be pregnant.'

Sophie heard his response and froze in her tracks. So bewitched had she been by the wonder of his lovemaking, his proposal, it had never crossed her mind she might get pregnant. How could she have been so dumb and blind? It was obvious Max had realised the implication of unprotected sex straight away. Was that why he'd asked her to marry him? Was that the real reason for their secret engagement, which obviously wasn't secret where Gina was concerned? He had told Gina he had asked Sophie to marry him, and mentioned the words *careless* and *pregnant*, but the word *love*, the most important reason for marriage, had never passed his lips.

Sophie's heart squeezed in her chest and she had trouble breathing as pain sharp as a knife sliced through her. Max had told her he *adored* her, he had said she was *priceless*—but, sickeningly, she realised he had never once mentioned *love*.

Was the secrecy he had insisted upon less to do with informing her father and more to do with Max keeping her sweet until he discovered if she was pregnant?

'I might have guessed.' Gina's scornful voice cut through her tormented thoughts. 'I warned you not to do anything impulsive, but no. You reacted like most men do at the sight of a willing woman. Well, whatever happens, you can't marry her without telling her. She hardly knows you, and in my opinion she is far too young to marry anyway. She hasn't even finished her education. And she has the right to choose whether she wants to be involved in this situation. So if you don't tell her, I will.'

To Sophie, it was another nail in the coffin of all of her hopes, and that Max should submit to such a scolding from a woman without any comment stunned her. He thought very highly of Gina, that much was obvious, and she had to be very sure of her standing in his life to lecture him in such a way.

'Sophie might be dumb enough to fall into bed with you—what girl wouldn't? Even I can't keep count of the number. I've given up trying,' Gina drawled angrily. 'But from what you have told me about her academic achievements she cannot be that stupid. She would soon guess something was wrong if her new husband kept disappearing from the marital home on a regular basis, probably overnight, and then when he did return did not have the energy to make love—which we both know is almost inevitable.'

'I will tell her—I will,' Max declared. 'But not yet. It has only been a couple of days.'

'Ah, Max, I do love you. But you are a typical man— impossible!' Gina replied.

'I know,' he chuckled, 'and I love you. I don't know what I would do without you. But look on the bright side—with any luck I may not need to tell Sophie anything at all.'

Suddenly, with blinding clarity, Sophie saw it all.

Marnie had been right. Max and Gina were lovers, and the only reason Max had proposed marriage to Sophie was because he might have made her pregnant. He had never even mentioned the possibility to *her*, his so-called fiancée, and tellingly she realised he had been careful to use protection every other time. What did he intend to do? She answered her own question—wait and see. And if she wasn't pregnant he would use her, then drop her like he did all the other women in his life.

If she *was* pregnant the pair of them were discussing how Sophie might handle their ongoing love affair as the pregnant wife left at home. She couldn't even blame Gina. She was all for telling the truth; it was Max who was the devious, lying one of the pair.

Pain and anger such as she had never felt in her life before consumed her. Tears pressed against the backs of her eyes, but she refused to let them fall. She wanted to rage and scream at the man who had seduced her so completely, stolen her heart and her innocence. How could she have thought he loved her? She was as dumb as Gina had said she was for falling for Max's charm, and the knowledge was soul destroying.

It took every bit of will-power she possessed to carry on walking to the entrance of the clearing. Maybe, just maybe, she was mistaken and there was some other explanation, her foolish heart cried. But the sight that met her eyes was the death of any hope that she might be wrong.

They were sitting on the bench, their arms around each other, their whole body language screaming long-term intimacy, and her heart turned to stone in her chest.

From somewhere she got the strength to move forward, and it was pride and pride alone that allowed her to declare, 'You are right, Max—you don't need to say a word. I heard everything, and—' *You don't need to marry me.* But she never got the chance to say it as Max cut her off.

'You heard everything?' He jumped to his feet. 'I'm sorry. I should have told you the truth. I didn't mean you to find out this way.' He walked towards her, a regretful, almost shameful smile on his handsome face. But she held up a hand to ward him off.

'No need to be sorry…. Gina's right. I am far too young to marry, and your situation does not appeal to me at all. I am leaving at the end of the week anyway, as my two months are up, so I'll say goodbye now. And wish you luck.'

'No, Sophie, you can't mean that!' he said, reaching for her. She took a step back; she couldn't bear for him to touch her. 'It is not as bad as it seems. Come and sit down, and we can talk it over with Gina. '

Not as bad! Disgust curled her mouth. It probably *wasn't* that bad in their sophisticated, decadent world, and that realisation was enough to numb all feeling in Sophie. 'No.' She shook her head, her green eyes glistening with anger, sliding contemptuously over him from head to toe. Her hero…her lover… The conniving, lying rat actually had the gall to suggest she sit down with him and his lover and discuss—what? A three-way relationship? Career woman or not, parental disapproval…whatever! Why Gina put up with him she had no idea.

'I have heard it all and there is nothing more to say. It was an interesting experience, but under the circumstances not one I wish to continue. I am not in the least interested in the kind of future you have mapped out, and luckily for me I discovered today there is no chance I am pregnant, so you have nothing to worry about except yourself.' She almost added *as usual*.

Max had never really cared about her. Even his love for Gina was not something Sophie recognised as true love. And she finally realised Max was the most arrogant, manipulative, selfish man she had ever had the misfortune to meet.

Sophie saw him straighten his massive shoulders and tense. For a second she imagined she saw a flash of raw pain in his dark eyes, but she must have been mistaken because when he looked at her his handsome face was a taut, expressionless mask.

'You are not the girl I thought you were. And you're right, there is nothing more to say—except there is no need for you to stay until the end of the week. Please oblige me by packing as soon as possible. I will square it with Alex and have your flight tickets waiting at the desk. I never want to set eyes on you again.'

Thinking about their parting now, Sophie saw again the hostility in Gina's eyes, and the hard, cold anger in Max's, and wondered why she had let the memory bother her for so long. They deserved each other, and she was well out of it. As for meeting Max for lunch—not likely… And on that defiant thought she finally fell asleep.

But the next day, at the end of the morning conference, as she was deep in conversation with the organiser, Tony

Slater, her defiance dipped when Max Quintano suddenly appeared in the foyer.

'Sophie.' He nodded his head in her direction and held out his hand to Tony Slater. 'Good to see you again, Tony. Sorry I could only make the dinner and not the meeting, but I hear the conference has been a great success. I believe that some very positive ideas have been formulated, which may be put into practice in the future. Maybe we can get together and discuss it further?'

Sophie's mouth fell open in shock. She could not believe the nerve of the man, interrupting their conversation, but if the expression on Tony's face was anything to go by *he* could not believe his luck—the great Max Quintano, suggesting a one-to-one, with *him!*

'Yes, that would be great.' Tony beamed, much to Sophie's disgust.

Max's dark triumphant eyes flicked mockingly over her and he chuckled softly as he addressed Tony again. 'Sophie and I are old friends and I am taking her out for lunch. I believe there are only closing speeches this afternoon, so please do me a favour and make Sophie's apologies to any interested parties for her early exit from the conference. I would like to show her something of Venice before she leaves tomorrow.' Withdrawing a card from his pocket, Max added, 'This is my number. Give me a call in the morning and we can arrange a meeting.'

Sophie tried to object; she had to fulfil her contract, and that meant staying until the end. But with the organiser of the conference declaring it was not necessary, that he would square it with her clients, before Sophie knew what had happened Max's hand was at her elbow and he was leading her out of the hotel. A male conspiracy if ever there was one, Sophie thought bitterly, with the sound of Tony's eager suggestion to enjoy her lunch ringing in her ears.

She shrugged off Max's hand as soon as they made the pavement and spun around to face him. 'I suppose you think you're clever, manipulating Tony Slater into excusing my absence? Where do you get off, interfering in my work?' she snarled, so angry she wanted to hit him.

He was staring down at her from his great height, all arrogance and powerfully male. The autumn sun was gleaming on his black hair and highlighting his chiselled features. Clad all in black—black jeans and a black cashmere sweater—he looked like the devil himself, she thought. But she was too mad to be frightened of him.

'Well, I have news for you, Quintano: I am *not* having lunch with you. Not today, not ever.' And, pulling her shoulder bag a little tighter over her shoulder, she added facetiously, 'But, hey, thanks for the day off.' And, swinging on her heel, she walked away.

Max let her go, because she was moving in the right direction. His motor launch was tied up fifty yards along the canal, and, although he was quite prepared to drag her kicking and screaming onto the launch, watching Sophie stride along was a lot more interesting. Her hair was loosely pinned with a mother-of-pearl clip at the nape of her neck and flowed like a curtain of pale silk down her back. Her pert bottom in a slim-fitting, short navy wool skirt was a pleasure to watch, and her legs—covered, he guessed, in silk stockings—were a pure joy.

Sophie didn't look back—she didn't dare! She was marching along the side of the canal, congratulating herself on her easy escape, when suddenly an arm snaked round her waist and she was lifted bodily into the air. She let out a surprised yell and began to struggle—only to be dumped unceremoniously onto a leather seat in the back of a boat. Before she could rise fully to her feet Max started the engine and cast off, which sent her crashing into the bottom of the vessel.

'You're crazy,' she yelled at Max's broad back. 'Stop this boat this minute, or I will have you arrested for kidnapping!' And to her utter astonishment, he did. She heard the engine die and, lifting her head, saw that Max had turned around and was leaning against the wheel, gazing down at her, his handsome face hard.

'If anyone is to be arrested it will be your father, Nigel Rutherford, for fraud.'

What the hell was he talking about now? Sophie thought furiously, tilting back her head to face him. A frisson of fear slid down her spine at the implacable intent in the cold black depths of the eyes that clashed with hers as he added, 'Unless you do exactly as I say.'

'You're mad! You can't threaten me or my father,' she blustered. Suddenly she recalled Max's comment last night about her family. She had thought nothing of it at the time, but now she wasn't so sure. Unease stirred inside her—how did he know her father was married again and had a son?

'I don't have to,' he responded calmly.

'Then why?' she asked, and stopped. She could read nothing in his austere features, but she knew for a fact that her father did not know Max. When she'd returned from Italy seven years ago her father had asked her if she'd enjoyed the break. In the conversation that followed he had revealed he had only met the owner, Andrea Quintano once, but he knew Alex. She supposed Alex might have mentioned her father's marital state. She had to wonder what else Alex might have mentioned.

Did Max know something about her dad's business? Was there something wrong? The tension between Margot and her father had been glaringly obvious at the weekend. Worriedly, she gnawed at her bottom lip—maybe they had money problems she knew nothing about. Dear heaven, the way Margot spent money it was certainly possible.

She was beautiful, Max acknowledged. With her skirt riding up around her thighs, her long legs splayed out in front of her, he saw he'd been right about the stockings— he could see the ribbons of her garter belt. The jacket of her suit was open, and the white silk blouse she wore underneath fitted over the high, firm curve of her breasts, revealing an enticing glimpse of cleavage that encouraged the eye to linger.

Reluctantly he raised his eyes to her face and saw the exact moment when she realised he was not joking. The angry glitter faded from her incredible eyes and her small white teeth nibbled at her full bottom lip. His body tightened—very soon *he* was going to nibble on her lush lips, and a lot more, and he did not intend to wait much longer.

'Because the law will, when his creditors get together next week,' he drawled sardonically. 'Unless I help you, of course—and that comes at a cost.'

'His creditors? And what do you mean—help *me*?' Suddenly realising she was at a distinct disadvantage sprawled at his feet, she struggled to sit up on the leather seat.

'I think you know. If you don't, have a guess,' he said with mocking cynicism, 'while I take us to lunch.' And with that he turned his back on her and started the engine.

For a moment Sophie stared at his back and wished she could stick a dagger in it, but it wasn't an option. Instead she ran their conversation over and over again in her head, and the more she thought the more worried and angry she became. But she did not dare argue with Max—not yet—not until she knew exactly what was going on.

Sitting on the edge of her seat, incapable of relaxing, she tried to focus on the beauty of her surroundings rather than the oppressive presence of Max at the wheel.

Venice in mid-October, cooler and with the worst crush of summer tourists gone, was a magical place. The sun-washed buildings edging the canals, the various crafts skimming through the water, the intricate bridges arching over the smaller canals—she should have been fascinated. And in any other circumstances she would have been. But she was too tense and too aware of Max to concentrate on anything.

CHAPTER FIVE

SOPHIE heard the tone of the engine change and, lifting her head, realised they were approaching a landing stage. She glanced up and saw a large, elegant pale-pink-washed house with a massive stone stairway leading up to it from two sides. She saw the huge double doors open and a man run down one side of the steps to catch the rope Max threw to him. Within seconds the launch was tied up.

She began to rise to her feet, and Max took her hand to help. She tried to pull free, but his fingers tightened. For a moment his eyes flared with anger, and when he spoke his voice was dangerously soft. 'Sophie, behave. I will not have you embarrassing me in front of my staff—understand?'

Glittering green eyes lifted to his. 'I don't want to be here. So we can solve both our problems if you just let me go,' she drawled facetiously. He had the nerve to laugh.

'Nice try, but no.' A moment later, with Max's arm firmly around her shoulders, she'd been introduced to Diego, his factotum, the man who had tied up the launch, and was walking up the steps to the impressive entrance doors, Diego leading the way.

The house was incredible; Sophie stood in the great entrance hall and simply stared.

The floor was a magnificent marble mosaic in cream and earthy tones, the walls magnolia, with elegant gold mouldings and works of art tastefully displayed all around. Marble columns formed a framework for the huge reception hall, an open door between two of them revealing a long dining table laid for lunch. She tilted her head back to look up at the ceiling and gasped at the centre dome, painted to rival the Sistine Chapel, and the huge chandelier that had to be Murano crystal. It took her breath away. The impressive steps outside were mirrored, and outclassed only by the fabulous marble staircase inside, which swept up to a central landing and divided again to a vast gallery that she presumed led to the bedrooms.

'Welcome to my home, Sophie.'

Awestruck, she glanced at Max. 'It's amazing!' she exclaimed. 'But I never knew you lived in Venice.' The Quintano family had been a constant source of gossip in the hotel when she'd worked there. She knew Max had an apartment in Rome, but no one had ever mentioned Venice. If she had known she would never have set foot in the city.

'When we first met I had just bought this place. It was a rundown *palazzo,* and I had it faithfully restored to its original style. Do you like it?'

'Like it? You are joking—it's fabulous.' She smiled, forgetting her animosity towards him for the moment, but she was brutally reminded of it two seconds later.

'Good. Then you will have no problem with living here for a while,' he said smoothly.

'Wait just a damn minute. I—' She never got the chance

to reiterate that she didn't even want to stay for lunch, because he pulled her possessively into his arms.

His dark eyes glittered golden with some fierce emotion, and his mouth settled on hers with a passionate intensity that caught her completely off guard. She flattened her hands against his chest, trying to push him away, but he simply pulled her tighter against him so she could not move. It was a kiss like nothing she had experienced before—a ravaging, possessive exploration that horrified her even as she shuddered at the fierce sensations he awakened.

Sophie closed her eyes and tried to will her body not to respond. As the kiss went on and on and he plundered her mouth, one hand swept feverishly up and down her spine, urging her into ever closer contact with his hard thighs. His other hand dipped below the neckline of her blouse to cup her breast, long fingers slipping beneath the lace of her bra to stroke a burgeoning nipple. An ache started low in her stomach and snaked down to her loins as a long-forgotten passion ran like wildfire through her veins.

When he finally allowed her to breathe, she was gasping for air, shaking all over with the shock of her arousal. He didn't give her time to recover but began to trail kisses down her throat, sucking on the vulnerab hollow where her pulse beat madly.

She never heard the discreet cough, only felt head lifting and glanced up to see anger and mingling beneath his heavy-lidded eyes as he t they'd be there in a few minutes.

'What do you think you are playing at?' s fighting for breath and trying to move without much success.

'Tasting the merchandise,' Max said with brutal honesty. 'If I am going to bail your father out of debt, then I need to know it will be worth my while.'

Finally the penny dropped, and she realised his *living here* comment made horrible sense. Sophie looked at him with wide, appalled eyes. 'You actually imagine I will stay with you to get my father out of a fix?' she murmured. 'That is what all this is about?' She shook her head as if to clear it, fury rising inside her to give her eyes a wild glitter. 'Sorry to disappoint you, but my father is a grown man. If he is in any trouble—which I very much doubt—he is old enough to get out of it on his own,' she said with bitter sarcasm, hating Max with a depth of feeling that was almost frightening.

'He is your father. You should know.' He set her free and she took an unsteady step back, relieved he had given up on his demeaning proposition. But her relief was short lived. 'Maybe being bankrupted will do him good—though how it will affect your young brother remains to be seen.' He shrugged. 'But you probably know that better than I.'

'How dare you!' Sophie was goaded to retaliate at the cruel taunt. 'You make me sick. If my father needed my help I would give him all I have, even if I had to find ways of doing it. But

Max's ... desire old Diego

... he demanded, ... out of his arms

... ly on her flushed furious ... your father only has a few ... ng. You should also know I ... go from your friend Abe. He ... th you and he asked me to say ... me to look after you. Of course

I said I would. Apparently he's flying to the Caribbean to join his wife and family on his yacht. So if you're counting on running to him for money, forget it.'

She swallowed the sudden lump that rose in her throat. How like Abe to put his mischievous oar in. She wouldn't mind betting he was laughing all the way across the Atlantic. But *she* wasn't laughing. Anger raged inside her that Max had had the arrogance to tell Abe he would look after her—as though she was a parcel to be passed around. But with the fury came an underlying sadness that Max, whom she had once thought she loved, could happily live in such a moral vacuum.

'Nothing to say?' he asked smugly.

She shook her head in disgust. 'I take it you're not married yet?' He couldn't be. Surely not even Max would have the gall to bring her here if he was? 'But, just out of curiosity, what would Gina say if I did agree to your disgraceful proposition?'

'There is nothing she can say—though obviously she won't be very happy, after last time. But as my mistress you won't need to meet her.'

She almost pitied Gina. Max's callousness appalled her. For one wild moment she considered walking out of his house, taking a water taxi to her hotel and then the next flight back to England, back to sanity. But the thought of Timothy held her back.

Max Quintano was not the sort of man to make mistakes—at least not in business. Much as she would like to, it would be foolhardy to just assume he was wrong about her father and dismiss the man. She needed to know the facts.

Max saw the indecision on her beautiful face and knew what she was thinking. 'If you don't believe me, call your father and ask him.' He indicated the telephone on a console table. 'Be my guest.'

He wanted Sophie more than any other woman he had ever known, and he had finally faced that fact when fate had put her in his path again last night. It had made his blood boil to see her with Abe Asamov, to see what she had become. The idea of the fat Russian enjoying her body—a body that *he* had initiated into sex—had sent a totally alien streak of possessively charged sexual desire raging through him.

Sophie was the only woman he had ever asked to marry him, but luckily he had discovered in time that she was the type to be economical with her wedding vows. As he recalled, the old English vow was *With all my worldly goods I thee endow.* She was obviously all for that but when it came to *in sickness and in health* she didn't want to know. She had dropped him like a shot when she'd heard he might have cancer.

It had taken him a while to recover from the cancer, and it had taught him to be a lot more circumspect in his sex life. But it hadn't stopped him wanting Sophie in the most basic way the minute he had set eyes on her again. Sexual desire took no account of the character, or lack of it, in the object of desire. It was simply there, twisting his gut.

He had denied it for seven years, because seven years ago he'd had more to worry about than her betrayal, but now he was damned if he was going to let her get away with deserting him unscathed. Now he was going to indulge his passion until the desire faded and he could look at her with nothing but the contempt she deserved.

Sophie looked at him standing before her, overpowering and arrogantly male, with an aura of silent, deadly strength that was decidedly threatening. 'I'll use my cellphone,' she said, determined to exert what little bit of control she had left over the situation. 'And I would like some privacy.'

'I will wait for you in the dining room,' Max drawled, and she watched him turn before she retrieved her cellphone from her bag.

Sophie switched off her phone and switched off her life, as she knew it, for the foreseeable future.

Surprisingly, she had contacted her father easily at home. When she'd told him she had bumped into Max Quintano at dinner last night, and he had told her there were rumours in the hotel trade that his company was in trouble, her dad had been amazingly frank. A group of creditors *were* due to meet next Monday, varying from airlines to hoteliers. Apparently he had delayed payment of clients' money and spent it.

He'd been sure he could put it right if he sold the house and rented something small until he had a chance to straighten out his business, but Margot hadn't accepted the fact so he had been trying to raise money from the banks. Last week Margot had finally accepted the house had to be sold, but she wasn't happy about it. The reason he was at home in the middle of the day was because he was expecting the estate agent.

Hence the atmosphere last weekend, Sophie thought bitterly, moving reluctantly towards the dining room. Her father's last comment was ringing in her head: 'I'm sure

I can convince the creditors to hold off until I sell up, but whatever you do, don't upset Max Quintano. His father died a few months ago, and it was only when he looked into the family business that the discrepancies in payment came to light. If he had left his mother, who ran it with her husband for the last few years, in sole charge then this would not have happened so fast.'

Her father had never had a high opinion of women in the business world. Being such a chauvinist, it was surprising he allowed Margot to push him around.

She entered the dining room. Max was sitting at the top of a long table, with the light from the window catching the silver streaks in the gleaming blackness of his neatly styled hair. No sign of the errant locks that used to fall over his brow, or the teasing brilliant smile that had haunted her dreams long after she'd left him.

He had changed; he was leaner, harder, more aloof. But he could still make her pulse race just by looking at her. Sophie's stomach muscles clenched into a tight knot of tension as she stared down the length of the table at him.

'Did you speak to your father?' he asked.

'Yes.' She made herself walk forward until she reached the place-setting Diego had laid on Max's right. 'And you are correct.' She watched as he rose and pulled out the chair for her, ever the gentleman. She almost laughed at the hypocrisy of the man; why treat her like a lady when he was intent on turning her into little better than a prostitute? But she said nothing and sat down.

'I usually am,' he drawled, arrogantly resuming his seat, and at that moment Diego entered with a champagne bucket and placed it beside Max. 'Thank you, Diego. I will do the honours.' Taking the bottle, he uncorked it expertly and filled the two fluted glasses on the table. He held one out to Sophie.

'Take it, Sophie. A toast to old friends and renewed lovers,' he said sardonically.

'I haven't agreed to anything,' Sophie protested, but it was a weak protest and he knew it.

'Your very presence at this table tells me you have agreed,' he declared, his eyes lit with mocking amusement 'Otherwise you would have been out of this house in a heartbeat.'

He was right, damn him! Hot, angry bitterness swept through her, but she was not prepared to give up without a fight. 'My father is putting the family home on the market as we speak. Given time, he can clear his debts,' she said defiantly. But deep down she knew she wasn't going to see her little brother homeless and her father ruined.

'He does not have time,' Max asserted softly, his firm mouth twisting with cynical derision. 'I made sure of that this morning.'

'You... But how?' Sophie demanded tensely, green eyes flaring across the table at him.

'I had a very productive morning and bought out your father's creditors. I am now his sole creditor, and as such his fate is in my hands.' An ebony brow arched sardonically. 'Or yours...'

'You swine!' she exclaimed. 'You really expect me to sleep with you to pay my father's debt?'

'Sleep is not what I have in mind,' he said with silken emphasis. 'And outraged virtue ill becomes you when I know Abe Asamov was the most recent in no doubt a long line of lovers.' Dark, insolent eyes mocked her fierce tension, and he lifted the glass again. 'Take this. You look like you need it.'

Sophie could feel angry colour rising in her cheeks at his casual destruction of her character. But with her father's warning ringing in her head she fought back the fury that threatened to engulf her and took the glass he offered from his outstretched hand. The slight graze of his fingers on hers made her flinch, and her skin tingled with a multitude of sensual yearnings that shamed and inflamed her. She raised the glass to her lips and took a large swallow of the sparkling liquid—she *did* need it!

Max was so damn arrogant, so confident in his ability to get what he wanted in business and in his private life. Look at the way Gina still clung to him. Yet he must have hurt her a thousand times with his decadent lifestyle—a lifestyle he was intent on dragging Sophie into.

'No argument, Sophie?' he queried, leaning back in his chair, the trace of a satisfied smile quirking his wide mouth.

She affected a casual shrug, but inside she was seething with a mixture of emotions—the uppermost a burning desire to knock the smug look off his face. 'I don't believe in fighting. A reasoned debate is more my style,' she said coolly.

'So sensible, Sophie,' Max opined mockingly. 'But are you able to pay your father's debt by next Monday?' he demanded, his challenging gaze capturing hers.

Tension crackled in the air, and suddenly Sophie felt seriously threatened. He quoted a figure slightly over a million, and she stared at him in mute horror. The amount was nothing to a man of his wealth, but a fortune to most people—herself included. The house in Surrey had been the family home for thirty years and, given the astronomical rise in property prices in London and the home counties recently, the sale might fetch that much, but her father would be left with next to nothing.

Minutes earlier she had been determined to play it cool, but now every vestige of colour drained from her beautiful face.

'I take your silence as a no. And, that being the case, you will agree to be my lover until such time as I tire of you or your father repays me.'

'Not if…*when,*' Sophie asserted vehemently, but a chill was invading her body, and with it the growing certainty that she had no escape. How long would it take to sell the house in Surrey? she wondered. Set in an acre of garden, it was a highly desirable residence, with five bedrooms and five bathrooms, thanks to Margot's expensive modernization. The irony of the situation didn't escape her. It was an easy commute to London, and it should sell quickly.

How hard could it be to have Max as a lover for a month or two, maybe three? Millions of women would leap at the chance…. If she could get over the fact she despised the man it might even cure her of her helpless physical reaction to him. Then afterwards she could move on with her life and maybe meet and marry a decent man, have a family….

'Then we are agreed?'

Reluctantly she nodded her head, just as Diego arrived with a silver platter and proceeded to serve the meal.

She picked at the mushroom risotto, her stomach churning in sickening protest at the bits she tried to swallow. The veal cutlet that followed she ignored, while Max tucked in to everything with obvious enjoyment. The only words spoken were a few conventional comments on the food. On the inside Sophie was almost overwhelmed with a sense of frustrated anger at her situation, and her hatred of Max was building with every passing minute.

'More wine? Or would you prefer coffee?' Max asked. 'Then we can get down to business.'

She glanced at her half-empty glass, realising she had drunk too much already on a near empty stomach, and clipped back, 'Nothing, thank you.'

'I must say, Sophie, you have surprised me,' he said, subjecting her to a long, lingering scrutiny that roamed over her face and then down, to pause over the proud thrust of her breasts. 'I didn't think you would accept my proposition quite so quickly.'

The arrogant devil knew damn well that she'd had to. With her nipples hardening simply at his glance, she was shamed and furious at the same time.

She had dated and kissed a few other men over the years, but none had aroused her enough to want to do anything more. Yet with just a look this man could make her body react like the dumb teenager she had once been. It wasn't fair.... But then life wasn't fair, she thought bitterly, or she wouldn't be here now. She glanced at him, big, dark and dangerous. A couple of hours in close proximity to Max had strained her nerves to the limit, but he was so arrogantly sure of himself that she decided to strike back.

'Well, as you said, Abe has left for the Caribbean, and my father tells me time is of the essence.' She smiled slightly and deliberately let her eyes roam slowly over him before adding, 'You're not a bad alternative, I suppose.' She drained her glass. 'Now, as you said, we should get down to the nitty-gritty.' Filled with Dutch courage, she continued, 'As well as settling my father's money problems, I would like to know how much you are going to pay *me*. I have a well-paid job, and I stand to lose a lot if I have to hang around with you. I'm not sure of the going rate for a mistress, so I will have to trust your wealth of knowledge on the subject.' She saw his thunderous frown and warmed to her theme. 'Do I have to stay here, or do I get my own apartment? I need to know all these things, and obviously I need it in writing.'

CHAPTER SIX

BAITING a man like Max Quintano was a stupid idea, Sophie realised almost immediately. To say her response had infuriated him was an understatement. He leapt to his feet, grabbed her wrist and hauled her to hers, then spun her around to face him in one fluid movement.

'*Dio*! You would tempt the devil himself with that smart mouth,' he grated, his dark eyes glittering with inimitable anger. 'You obviously need some training in how to be a mistress. For a start it is bad form to mention past lovers. My study—now.'

Sophie took a deep, steadying breath as he almost dragged her from the room and into another that was obviously his domain. Books lined one wall, and a state-of-the-art computer set-up stretched along another. There were armchairs either side of a large fireplace, and in front of the window there was a massive desk with a winged-back chair behind it.

His hand tightened briefly on her wrist, and then with a muffled oath he thrust her into an armchair. 'Stay there and don't move.' She cringed at the force of his barely leashed fury as he strode over to the desk and flung himself down in the hide chair. 'You want it all legal? Then that is what you shall have,' he declared, and picked up the telephone.

An hour later he dropped a document on her lap, but Sophie was past caring. She was thoroughly disgusted with the whole affair. She had always known Max was a ruthless man, but she had never realised quite how brutally blunt he could be.

He had called his lawyer and the man had appeared within fifteen minutes. The following conversation had been the most shaming in her life. Max, as her father's only creditor, had agreed not to demand payment of the debt and bankrupt the company if in return Sophie would live with him until he decided to end the arrangement. At that point the debt would be wiped out. In other words, Sophie was the collateral for her father's debt. At her insistence, a clause had been added to say that she was free to go immediately if her father repaid the debt. This clause was unnecessary, according to the lawyer, but she didn't trust Max an inch.

She had tried to brazen it out, and had suggested again that men usually provided a mistress with an apartment, and did not have her living in their own home. Only to have Max respond that with her track record he didn't trust her out of his sight. She had shut up after that.

The lawyer had presented the finished document and signed it, and witnessed her total humiliation along with Max. But she had signed it, so what did that make her?

'Satisfied?' a laconic voice drawled, and she looked up to see Max towering over her like some great avenging angel.

Getting to her feet, she picked up her shoulder bag. 'Yes, you have made my position perfectly clear. Now, if you don't mind, I need to go back to the hotel and consult my diary, make some calls and rearrange my schedule for a week or two. I'll get back to you tomorrow,' she informed him coldly.

'No. You can do that from here. Now it is time for *my* satisfaction.' Without another word he swung her into his arms and carried her up the stairs, oblivious to the blows she landed on his broad chest.

'Put me down,' she snapped. 'I am quite capable of walking.'

'You're not getting the chance,' he asserted as he shouldered open a door and lowered her slowly down the long length of his body until her feet touched the floor. 'Because your first lesson as my live-in lover starts here,' he declared, his dark gaze hard and chilling in its intent as he closed the door behind him. 'A mistress is always ready and willing for her man.' He reached for her, his hands catching her shoulders. 'And she never strikes him.' He paused. 'Unless asked to in the pursuit of pleasure of course,' he mocked.

In that moment the enormity of what she had agreed to finally hit her. She glanced wildly around the luxuriously appointed room, her eyes widening in fear at the enormous bed. 'Oh, my God. What have I done?' she groaned, her gaze lifting to the man holding her.

'Nothing, so far.' His sensuous lips curved in a sardonic smile. 'But that is about to change.' He pushed her further into the room and stopped by the bed. 'Take off your jacket,' he demanded, his hands sliding down her shoulders to the curve of her hips. 'And the rest—except for the garter belt. I rather like the idea of removing that myself.'

'How do you know—?' But he cut her off with a finger to her lips.

'Sprawled in the boat. But no more questions now.' He moved back and sat down on the edge of the bed. 'I want to inspect the goods and see if you are worth what I am paying.'

He wanted to humiliate her—as if he hadn't done that enough already. But for the first time in hours Sophie began to think clearly and wonder why. She let her gaze roam over him. He was aggressively male, with a fantastic physique and rugged good looks; he could have any woman he wanted. So why blackmail her into his bed? Because basically that was what he had done, by using her love for her family against her. Why was he so mad about it?

They had parted years ago. She supposed technically she had jilted him, but under the circumstances he had nothing to complain about. Yet she could sense the latent anger lying beneath his apparent casual control and she could see no reason for it—unless it was some dubious desire for revenge. Maybe she had bruised his ego by walking out on him—not many women would, if any— but why bother after seven years?

'Did you plan this? Did you know I was going to be in Venice?' She asked the questions she should have done at the beginning, her gaze lifting to his, searching for the truth.

'No,' he said smoothly, and the expression in the eyes that held hers was contemplative. 'The first time we met, my brother had died four months earlier. This time my father died four months ago. The Japanese consider the number four unlucky—the devil's number. I am not superstitious, but you seem to have a knack of appearing in my life after a tragedy.' He shrugged his broad shoulders. 'Fate or sheer chance—take your pick. I saw you with Asamov, looking more beautiful than ever and obviously more experienced, and—knowing the state of Nigel Rutherford's finances—I decided to have you.'

'And that is why you are doing this?' She drew a deep, unsteady breath, a snippet of conversation from years ago coming back to her.

Gina had told him she'd warned him not to do anything impulsive when he had revealed he might have got Sophie pregnant. Max obviously hadn't changed that much—he still took what he wanted on a whim. Suddenly she felt heart sick, because the really sad thing was that deep down, in the sensual part of her being, a part she had denied for years, was a secret longing to be back in his arms…and even now she didn't want to believe he was as cruelly amoral as he appeared.

Max saw the puzzlement in her eyes, noted the pallor of her face and grimaced. She looked like some virgin being led to the sacrificial altar. Hell! She was doing it to him again—tricking him with her aura of innocence when underneath she had the heart of a bitch.

A cynical smile twisted his lips. 'I'm not doing anything. I am waiting for you to perform.'

Who was she trying to kid? Max had no finer feelings. Well, if he wanted a whore he could have one.

Fuelled by anger, she shrugged off her jacket and slipped the blouse from her shoulders. She unzipped her skirt and shimmied out of it, and stood hands on hips brazenly before him. 'Do you like what you see?' she prompted scathingly. He could look, but she was damned if she was going to lie down and surrender without a fight.

Max more than liked it… Her lush breasts were cradled in gossamer white lace, high-cut white lace shorts—so much more sexy than a common thong—enhanced her incredibly long legs, and the matching garter belt was all he had imagined and more.

He lifted his gaze to her face. 'So far, I do.' She looked sinfully sexy, her green eyes glittering with defiance, and slowly he rose to his feet. 'Except the picture is not quite right. The rest has to go—but first…' he reached for her shoulders and curved one hand around her neck '…*this* has to go.' Deftly he unfastened the clip that held her hair and ran his fingers through the pale silken mass. 'I prefer your hair loose.' He pulled the soft strands down over one shoulder and traced the length over her breast. 'Try to remember that.'

A shiver snaked down Sophie's spine and she tensed, her moment of bravado over, suddenly fiercely aware of his hand on her bare shoulder, the knuckles of his long fingers grazing her breast. 'Yes,' she murmured, lowering her eyes from his intense gaze, appalled at the ease with which her body responded to his slightest touch.

'*Yes* is good.' He drew her closer. 'You're learning fast,' and Max was fast losing what little control he had left.

She felt his fingers gripping her shoulders and glanced up through the shield of her lashes to his mobile mouth. She knew he was going to kiss her.

She wouldn't respond. She would *not,* Sophie silently vowed, her hands curling into fists at her sides. But when his lips found hers her resolve was strained to the limit. His kiss was hungry, punishing, and passionate. She didn't struggle, but neither did she respond. He lifted his head, his hands dispensing with her bra, and she stifled a groan as he palmed her breast.

'There is no escape now, Sophie. You will only delay the inevitable and hurt yourself in the process if you try to deny me.'

His voice was implacable, and a shiver ran through her. Max saw this and snaked an arm around her waist. He drew her against him, his mouth finding hers again, and he kissed her with such power that it made her senses swirl. Together, the caress of his hand against her bare breast and the demanding power of his mouth conspired to defeat her resistance, and helplessly her traitorous body surrendered to the heat of arousal surging through her.

A whimpering cry escaped as his mouth left hers to bite the curve of her neck, his hand stroking over her full breast, cupping the firm flesh with his fingers, teasing the sensitive peaks into aching buds of need. He lifted his head, his dark eyes burning down at her, and she grabbed his shoulders, afraid she would fall as her bones turned to water. But the arm around her waist held her firm, his fingers edging beneath her lace briefs.

'I swore I would make you strip, make you squirm,' he rasped. 'But somehow it does not seem important any more.'

She saw the savagery in his glittering gaze and for a second she was afraid. But with a low groan Max captured a rigid rosy nipple in his mouth and she was past all conscious thought. He licked and suckled with tormenting tender bites that sent quivering arrows of need cascading through her body.

'Yes, tremble for me,' Max grated and, lifting her off her feet, he swung her onto the bed and wrenched her briefs down her long legs. 'This is how I pictured you,' he growled, his eyes devouring her. The white lace garter belt and silk stockings were her only covering, and her glorious hair tumbled around her shoulders. Desire raged through him, and swiftly he dragged off his clothes, all the time feasting his eyes on the sensual splendour of her spread out before him.

Breathless and lying on her back, Sophie widened her eyes in helpless fascination on his tall tanned body. He was totally aroused—all hard, urgent male, and she wanted him with the same passion, the same eagerness, as the first time they'd made love. She knew later she would hate him again, but now she was not even embarrassed by their nudity.

'Look all you like,' Max said, with a low, husky laugh of masculine pleasure as he knelt on the bed beside her. He reached to brush her hair from her shoulders, and somehow his words hit a nerve—was she still so obvious to him?

'I will—and don't forget protection,' she said, in an attempt to reassert some control, remembering the first time she'd been with him and the awful aftermath. 'I want no repercussions from this sordid affair.'

'I'm not that careless. I don't know where you have been,' he lashed back. For a second his hands tightened on her shoulders, his dark eyes blazing down at her with a contempt he did not try to hide. He felt a primitive determination to drain every ounce of satisfaction from her exquisite body, to imprint his mastery over her so all her past lovers faded into oblivion. But first he reached for the bedside table and protection.

'Be my guest,' he drawled, sinking back on his knees and holding it out to her.

'I…' She stretched out her hand and then dropped it. 'No…you.' And the heat that coloured her skin was not so much sexual as a total body blush.

He offered her a mocking smile and leant over her to brush the hair away from her brow. He saw the tumult in her green eyes. 'Not so forward now.' Actually, Max was amazed she could still blush—but it didn't make any difference to the need pounding away in his blood, the need to dominate and captivate this sexy siren who had haunted his dreams for far too long. With that in mind, he dipped his head to claim her mouth, all of her…

At the touch of his lips on hers Sophie was once again swept away on a wave of sensuality. His tongue tasted her mouth, and when the need to breathe moved him his lips brushed down her throat and bit gently on the madly beating pulse he found there, then moved lower to her taut breasts.

She touched him then, letting her hands slide over his shoulders to feel the tension in his mighty body. She stroked her fingers down his back, lost in the wonder of him, of his satin-smooth skin beneath the pads of her fingers. His tongue licked her breast and she groaned, her fingers digging into his skin as he took the aching bud into his mouth and suckled with fierce pleasure, first one and then the other. The feel of his tongue, hot and wet, sent a renewed explosion of passion though every part of her.

Max lifted his head and knelt back, so her hands fell

from his body. He stared down at her, his heavy-lidded eyes glinting with fiercely leashed desire.

'Patience, *bella mia*.' His hands stroked tantalisingly slowly up from her ankles over her silk-clad legs to settle on her thighs. He parted them and moved between her legs, bending his dark head to kiss the band of naked skin above her stockings, and she groaned out loud, her thighs quivering at the subtle caress. She needed to touch him and tried to rise, but Max placed a hand on her stomach and pushed her back down. 'Not yet.'

Helplessly Sophie watched him gaze down at her naked thighs, at the golden curls guarding her femininity, with dark, intense eyes. His fingers slipped beneath the two white suspenders, flicking them open with hands that were not quite steady, then very slowly he peeled the stockings down her legs. And then just as slowly, with hands and mouth, he stroked and kissed his way back up, until she was a trembling mass of mindless sensation.

She gasped as his fingers reached the short golden curls to part the soft velvet folds beneath. His head dipped again, and she cried out as his teeth grazed the nub of her sex, then lost all control and gave herself up to the wondrous torment of his lips and tongue.

Her hands stretched out to clutch at his shoulders, her fingers feverishly stroking up into his thick black hair. She felt him tense and pull back.

'*Dio!* The taste of you is so sweet,' Max groaned, and slipped his hands beneath her thighs, kissing his way up her quivering flesh to her stomach, her breasts and finally her lips.

As his tongue plunged deep into her mouth he parted

her thighs wider and in one smooth thrust entered the hot, pulsing centre of her. Sophie winced at the slight pain— he was hard and thick, and it had been so long—but her legs and arms instinctively locked around him. And when he moved inside her time stopped. There was only the rapture, the ecstasy, of his awesome body possessing her.

She cried out as he moved in her with ever deeper powerful strokes, until she was sobbing his name over and over again. Her inner muscles clenched around his throbbing length as she was swept into a violent climax, and before her orgasm had time to subside he joined her, his great body shuddering uncontrollably with the powerful force of his release.

Max lay over her, his head on the pillow beside her, and Sophie held him, her slender hands stroking down his broad back, glorying in the weight, the scent of him, the heavy thud of his heart against her breast. For a while the real reason for her presence in his bed was completely forgotten. But she got a rude awakening when Max rolled over and slid off the bed.

Unashamedly naked, he stared down at her, his black eyes glinting with pure male satisfaction. 'The chemistry is still there—you still want me. That wasn't bad to begin with,' he drawled, in a deep, dark voice, and a chill invaded Sophie's bones at the mocking tone. 'But I never did get to take off your garter belt. Stay where you are until I get rid of this, and then we can continue.'

She watched him walk across to a door on the far side of the room—the bathroom, she guessed. The afternoon sun shone through the windows, gleaming on his big bronzed body, and stupid tears burnt the back of her eyes.

What had she expected? Tenderness? Caring…?

Blinking hard, she slid her legs off the bed and stood up.
No way was she going to wait for him like some besotted
fool. Been there, done that....

CHAPTER SEVEN

THE NEXT MORNING Sophie opened her eyes and yawned, and for a moment she was blissfully unaware of her surroundings and her situation. She stretched languorously and flinched, as muscles she hadn't known she had ached, reminding her of the humiliating truth. She had given herself to Max as she had done when she was nineteen— but it had been very different.

Because after seven years of celibacy, and with Max presuming she was vastly more experienced than she really was, he had subjected her to a lesson in eroticism and introduced things she had never imagined were possible. Worse still was the knowledge that she had responded with an eager mindless sexuality that she had no control over. She glanced across the huge bed. The only sign that Max had been there was an indentation in the pillow, and the lingering scent of him on the bedlinen and her body.

She drew in a deep, steadying breath and sat up, pulling the sheet around her neck. The clock on the bedside table said eight. She glanced warily around, as if she expected him to leap out at her at any moment.

She couldn't face him…not yet. Slowly she swung her legs off the bed and stumbled to the bathroom. She stepped into the huge circular shower stall and turned on the water, flinching as a dozen powerful jets pounded her body. She let her head fall back and closed her eyes—and a kaleidoscopic picture of the last twenty-four hours whirled in her head….

Max returning from the bathroom, his tautly muscled body still totally naked… The ease with which he had changed her mind and removed the garter belt… Her breasts swelled at the memory.

The tender lovemaking of her youth hadn't prepared her for the full force of Max's sexual expertise—or the wild woman she had become in his arms. She didn't know herself any more…. Turning off the shower, she stepped out and wrapped a bathsheet sarong-style around herself, and a smaller towel around her hair, then padded back into the bedroom.

She didn't want to think—to remember the humiliation when later Max had accompanied her back to the hotel to collect her belongings, or his brooding silence over dinner. When she had tried to speak, tried to assert some independence and insist she had to return to England to make arrangements for her apartment to be taken care of, he had coldly dismissed her suggestion and taken her back to the bed that was the scene of her earlier downfall.

At one point, buried deep inside her, driving her mad with a torturous pleasure, he had stopped. Sophie had begged him to continue, arching up, her nails digging desperately into his firm flesh, but he had resisted her every effort. And she had opened her eyes and registered the triumph in his molten black gaze, his taut features, as he'd grated, 'Did Abe make you feel like this?'

She'd given him the 'no' he wanted, and seen the glitter of masculine supremacy in his eyes as he took her over the edge.

Glancing at the rumpled bed now, she twisted her lips wryly as she recalled Max pointing out, as he'd left, that this was *her* bedroom. Where his was she had no idea. At least she didn't have to actually *sleep* with him, she thought, determined to try and be positive about their arrangement. But oddly the thought was not as much comfort as it should be.

Bending her head, she began to ferociously towel-dry her hair, in the hope of knocking every image of her shameful capitulation of him out of her mind.

'Here—let me do that.'

She jerked upright in surprise at the sound of his voice. 'Where did you come from?' she demanded. Six feet plus of arrogant male was standing in front of her, dressed casually in navy pants, a navy shirt and leather jacket. But to her shame the instant picture in her mind's eye was of the same body naked. His dark gaze met hers, and the gleam of sensual knowledge in his send a red tide of embarrassment over her pale face.

'I'm sure you would like to think I had sprung up from hell,' he drawled sardonically. 'But nothing so dramatic. This is the master suite. We share the bathroom and dressing room. I'm surprised you did not notice the connecting doors.'

Of course she had—the same way she'd seen the up-to-the-minute bathroom, all white and steel, with two

The Harlequin Reader Service® — Here's how it works:

Accepting your 2 free books and mystery gift places you under no obligation to buy anything. You may keep the books and gift and return the shipping statement marked "cancel." If you do not cancel, about a month later we'll send you 6 additional books and bill you just $3.80 each in the U.S., or $4.47 each in Canada, plus 25¢ shipping & handling per book and applicable taxes if any.* That's the complete price and – compared to cover prices of $4.50 each in the U.S., and $5.25 each in Canada – it's quite a bargain! You may cancel at any time, but if you choose to continue, every month we'll send you 6 more books which you may either purchase at the discount price or return to us and cancel your subscription.

*Terms and prices subject to change without notice. Sales tax applicable in N.Y. Canadian residents will be charged applicable provincial taxes and GST.

If offer card is missing write to: The Harlequin Reader Service, 3010 Walden Ave., P.O. Box 1867, Buffalo, NY 14240-1867

NO POSTAGE
NECESSARY
IF MAILED
IN THE
UNITED STATES

BUSINESS REPLY MAIL

FIRST-CLASS MAIL   PERMIT NO. 717-003   BUFFALO, NY

POSTAGE WILL BE PAID BY ADDRESSEE

HARLEQUIN READER SERVICE
3010 WALDEN AVE
PO BOX 1867
BUFFALO NY 14240-9952

OFFICIAL OPINION POLL

ANSWER 3 QUESTIONS AND WE'LL SEND YOU
2 FREE BOOKS AND A FREE GIFT!

0074823 | | | | | | | | | | | | |

FREE GIFT CLAIM # 3953

YOUR OPINION COUNTS!

Please check TRUE or FALSE below to express your opinion about the following statements:

Q1 Do you believe in "true love"?

"TRUE LOVE HAPPENS ONLY ONCE IN A LIFETIME."
○ TRUE
○ FALSE

Q2 Do you think marriage has any value in today's world?

"YOU CAN BE TOTALLY COMMITTED TO SOMEONE WITHOUT BEING MARRIED."
○ TRUE
○ FALSE

Q3 What kind of books do you enjoy?

"A GREAT NOVEL MUST HAVE A HAPPY ENDING."
○ TRUE
○ FALSE

YES, I have scratched the area below.

Please send me the **2 FREE BOOKS** and **FREE GIFT** for which I qualify. I understand I am under no obligation to purchase any books, as explained on the back of this card.

306 HDL EFV7

106 HDL EFUW

FIRST NAME

LAST NAME

ADDRESS

APT.#

CITY

STATE/ PROV.

ZIP/ POSTAL CODE

(HTF-P-06/06)

www.eHarlequin.com

DETACH AND MAIL CARD TODAY!

vanity basins and a massive circular pedestal bath. But it had not registered. In fact, nothing much had registered in her head since yesterday afternoon, except the dynamic, powerful presence of the man standing before her, and it had to stop.

But, before she could formulate a cutting response, Max took her unresisting hands from her head to slide them gently down her sides. Catching her shoulders, he pulled her close, and to her amazement began drying her hair.

For an instant she was tempted to rest her head on his broad chest and let him continue. But what little pride and self-respect she had left after her helpless surrender to him in the physical sense would not let her. Planting her hands on his chest, she pushed him away and he was left holding the towel.

'There is no need for that. I can use a hairdryer.'

His hooded eyes ran slowly over her wild tumbling hair, and lower, to the towel that slanted across her breasts. 'Need—maybe not. But want—well, *want* is a very compelling emotion.' To her surprise he chuckled, making a deep, sexy sound. 'And with that towel threatening to fall at any second, it is one emotion I am becoming very aware of.'

'What?' She glanced down and saw the towel sliding, and grabbed it up around her breasts as his arms captured her. His mouth came down to cover her own. She couldn't struggle, not without losing her only covering, and as his tongue stroked over hers she didn't want to. Her body melted against him as though tuned to his touch, and the familiar heat flared up inside her.

'Much as I would like to continue,' Max murmured, taking his mouth from hers, 'we have a flight to catch at ten.'

'A flight?' she exclaimed in confusion.

'Yes.' His hands fell from her. 'We have an appointment with your father for lunch. I arranged it last night, before dinner.' He looked at her stunned face with a gleam of mockery visible in his dark eyes. 'You have kept your part of the bargain more than adequately so far. Now I have to keep mine. But I want to meet the family who drove you to be so—obliging,' he said in a deep, cynical voice. Stepping back, he turned and walked over to the door, opened it, then stopped to fling over his shoulder, 'I'll see you downstairs in forty-five minutes. Don't keep me waiting,' and then left.

Sophie found the dressing room, and her few clothes neatly hanging in a wardrobe. It took her less than thirty minutes to get ready, she was so angry. After refusing her request yesterday, to return home to sort out her apartment, he had some nerve arranging to meet her family. But why was he doing it? To humiliate her further?

She gave a quick glance at her reflection in the mirror. Her hair was tied back with a red scarf, she'd applied minimum make-up and was wearing the same navy suit as yesterday. Someone had obviously pressed it, and, teamed with a red cotton top and flat red loafers, it gave a more casual effect. Her choice reflected her new status as a scarlet woman, she thought wryly—but she hadn't much choice. She had packed sparingly for her trip: a business suit, an evening dress and a selection of tops. The only casual item she had with her was a tracksuit she wore to run, or to lounge around in. Somehow she couldn't see the sophisticated Max appreciating his mistress in a track-suit. She tensed at the thought. When had her mind accepted she *was* his mistress?

She remembered reading the definition of the word in her mother's dictionary years ago, when Meg had mentioned her father's latest mistress. By definition a female *paramour*—a woman *courted* and beloved. If only, she grimaced. It certainly wasn't the connotation most people put on the word today—*kept and paid for* was the common assumption, and unfortunately in her case it was the truth.

Telling herself she didn't care, she straightened her shoulders and, with a defiant tilt to her chin, walked downstairs.

Max was waiting for her, and though she had told herself she would be perfectly composed, her stomach somersaulted as he let his gaze rake blatantly over her.

'A punctual woman.' His sensual mouth twisted with amusement. 'Or were you just keen to see me?' he mocked.

'No,' she said grimly. 'But I *am* keen to know why on earth you would want to meet my father with me in tow. Surely it's enough you will see him at the meeting next week? Even *you* can't be such a bastard as to tell him the truth about our arrangement.'

He shot out a powerful arm and yanked her against him. 'I've warned you before about your smart mouth.'

Sophie was trapped by the savage brilliance in his dark eyes. Her heart raced as his head dipped, taking her mouth in a deep, powerful kiss that was meant as a punishment.

She wanted to pull away, but the familiar musky scent of him teased her nostrils. Her toes curled with pleasure and with a will of their own her hands lifted to curl around his neck. She kissed him back, hungry for the taste of him. Then, without warning, he pushed her away.

'Call me all the names you want, but you *do* want me,' Max drawled, his dark eyes scanning her flushed face with cruel amusement. 'You worry too much.' He didn't bother to hide the derision in his tone as he added, 'Given the circumstances, your father will be delighted to see you, I have no doubt.'

'But what—?'

'What am I going to tell your father?' he said, reading her mind. 'The truth, of course.'

'Are you crazy?' she declared, eyeing him in horror. 'You can't possibly do that! He may not be the greatest dad in the world, but I *am* his daughter. He'd probably kill you!'

To her amazement, he laughed in her face. 'Ah, Sophie.' He shook his dark head. 'When I said the truth, I meant *my* version of it.' He reached an arm around her waist, and once again his dark head bent to take her mouth with his.

She shuddered beneath the brief, forceful passion of his kiss, and it took her a while to register what he was saying after he took his mouth from hers.

'We met and became *friends* years ago, in Sicily, and again in South America, and then again in Venice. For want of a better word—you are now my girlfriend, and as such I can't see you upset over your father when I can help…'

'You're definitely crazy. My father is not likely to believe that.' But bitterly she realised that Max was smart; there was just enough truth in his words to make them plausible.

'Yes, he is—because he will want to. I understand that as a widower he was quite a ladies' man, and spent generously on his woman. According to my information, his present wife costs him a fortune. I think we can safely say he will swallow the story whole, as long as you give me your full co-operation.'

Max was right about her father. In the years after her mother's death she would have had to be blind not to notice his penchant for the ladies. She had tried not to let it bother her, and mostly she had succeeded. How Max knew, she had no idea—and she wasn't sure she wanted to find out. In a way, they were two of a kind, she thought bitterly.

Letting none of her feelings show, she glanced coldly up at him and asked, 'What exactly do you mean by that?'

He grasped her chin between his fingers and looked deep into her eyes. 'You shall play the part of the eager and besotted lover—you did it once before to great effect, so you shouldn't find it too difficult. Especially after last night.' He pressed one last brief, punishing kiss on her mouth before, with her firmly held to his side, they walked out to where Diego waited with the launch.

An hour later Sophie, tense and trying to marshal her turbulent thoughts, sat in his private Citation X jet. According to Max, his enthusiasm evident, it was the world's fastest business jet, and could fly close to the speed of sound. It allowed up to eight people to travel the world and hammer out business deals at the same time. Talk about toys for the boys—multimillion pound toys, in this case, she thought dryly as the jet winged its way to London.

She glanced at Max in the seat next to her. He was wearing glasses and all his attention was on the papers he had withdrawn from a large briefcase—and had been since they took off, over an hour ago. Nervously she chewed on her bottom lip; they would be landing in another hour, and she still wasn't convinced the story Max had outlined to tell her father would work.

'Max,' she said beginning to panic, 'my father is not a fool—though he behaves like one at times,' she amended with feeling, still not able to fully grasp the ramifications of her dire situation. 'Are you sure…?'

His dark head turned towards her, and he slipped the glasses from his nose and rubbed his eyes.

'I never knew you wore glasses,' she said, diverted by his action.

'There is a lot you don't know about me, Sophie.' His mouth twisted cynically. 'But you have plenty of time to learn. As for your father, he will believe what we have already discussed. He is an experienced man with eyes in his head.' Curving a hand around her nape, he captured her mouth with his in a deep kiss. 'And you, Sophie, have the glow of a *satisfied* woman,' he drawled with silken satisfaction.

Did it show? Sophie wondered, flushing as she remembered last night. His last sentence effectively silenced her—as did the habit he seemed to have developed of kissing her without a second thought.

Seated to the left of her father, with Timothy beside her, Sophie tried her best to appear happy. But with Max and Margot opposite she was fast losing the will to live….

From the moment they had arrived from the airport by chauffeured limousine, and seen the 'For Sale' sign at the entrance to the drive, Sophie had been walking on eggshells. She'd had a brief respite when Timothy had demanded a ride in the limousine, and Sophie had gone with him while Max spoke privately with her father. She had shown the chauffeur the way to the village pub and back again, but when they had returned so had her tension.

Apparently Max had boldly announced to her father that he wanted to help him out of his present difficulties because he could not bear to see Sophie worried about her family, and a deal had been made.

Everyone was happy—especially Margot, who had taken one look at Max and started to flirt shamelessly. Max had cleverly fielded her innuendos and played the ardent suitor to perfection, keeping Sophie pinned to his side, and only letting her go when Margot had told them where to sit at the table.

Before the main course was finished, and after far too many personal questions from Margot, Max smoothly explained that he had had a soft spot for Sophie ever since he had first met her, when she was nineteen. He went to explain that they had met up again, purely by chance, in South America a few months ago—which wasn't strictly true. They *had* both been there; they'd just never met up.

Sophie could almost marvel at the way he avoided telling a direct lie, and when he said that their relationship had become serious in Venice, he turned his shining brown eyes to hers to add, 'Isn't that right, *cara*?'

'Yes.' What else could she say? She blushed scarlet at the gleam of mockery only she could see in Max's gaze, and that blush confirmed the story for her father.

It got worse when Margot asked her to help with coffee and cornered her in the kitchen.

'My goodness, you *are* a dark horse. I can't believe you've pulled a man like Max Quintano—but thank heaven you have. Play your cards right and he might even marry you. You want children, so get pregnant. That way even if he won't tie the knot you will be made for life.'

Sophie had often wondered if Margot had got pregnant deliberately, and now she knew—but she couldn't be angry because she loved Timothy so very much.

Sophie began to say, *I am quite happy with my life as it is*, but stopped, realising it would be a lie. She had only been happy until she had met Max again.

Margot shook her head and loaded the coffee tray. 'At least we get to keep the house. Whatever you do, don't upset the man until your father's debts are settled.'

'No, Margot, you don't understand. The house still has to be sold.'

'Don't be ridiculous. You're as bad as your father. Even if the house *is* sold, after the mortgage is paid off it won't make a fraction of what is owed. But for some reason Max fancies you—maybe you are good in bed.' She cast Sophie a brief doubting glance. 'I have heard he is a great lover. Maybe the attraction is in teaching you... But, whatever it is, one word from you and he will not see your family home sold to strangers. So start talking, quit worrying and pass me the cream and sugar.'

Trailing behind Margot back into the dining room, Sophie barely glanced at the others as she resumed her seat. She drank the coffee Margot poured without lifting her head. From the couple of months she had envisaged as being Max's mistress, her sentence seemed to have become open-ended. She knew that on the death of her mother the mortgage on the house had automatically been paid off by joint insurance—her father had told her so. It had never entered her head that he would remortgage it. How stupid was that? But with a young and expensive wife like Margot it was inevitable, and she supposed she should have guessed.

Barely two minutes after serving the coffee, Margot was leaning towards Max. 'More coffee, Max?' Her avid eyes were almost eating him alive. 'Let me fill you up—or perhaps you would prefer something else?' she prompted with an arch look, before adding, 'A cognac, or champagne to celebrate?'

Sophie could stand it no longer; she pushed back her chair and dragged Timothy out of his. 'Come on, Tim, you have sat still long enough. We will leave the adults to their drinks and go for a walk.' And she was out of the dining room and into the kitchen like a shot.

Opening the back door with Tim's hand in hers, she walked out into the crisp autumnal air. She took a few deep breaths, trying to cleanse her mind and her body from the shame she felt about what she had done and what was happening inside.

Tim tugged at her hand. 'Can we climb to the tree house?' he asked eagerly.

Looking down into his happy, innocent face, her heart swelled with love and she knew she had made the right decision. She would do anything to keep her brother in a happy home, with both parents, and if that meant saving her dad from bankruptcy, so be it….

Margot was young, attractive. Sophie didn't see her as the type to stay with a much older husband who was broke. Cynical, she knew, but realistic.

She smiled at Tim. 'Yes, of course, darling.' They set off down the path that wound round sculptured flowerbeds and manicured lawns to where a box hedge half hid the lower garden of fruit trees and pasture. A well-used child's swing and a slide stood in a clearing among the apple trees, and at the bottom was a hawthorn hedge with a large beech tree at the end. It had been Sophie's favourite place as a child. She had an abiding memory of her mother, pushing her high in the air on the swing, and sweeping her up in her arms as she careened to the foot of the slide.

Moisture hazed her eyes as they approached the beech tree and the rickety platform built across a fork in the trunk that Tim euphemistically called the tree house. Sophie had built it with her mother's help when she was eight. She had reinforced it last year. Now, giving Timothy a hand up, she climbed up behind him. Memories, she thought wistfully, looking at Tim's happy and excited face. They had no price. She knew she had done the right thing in accepting Max's dishonourable proposition.

'Really, Sophie, what must poor Max think? Climbing trees at your age.' Margot's tinkling laughter brought Sophie's attention down to the ground where Margot, clinging to Max's arm, was leading him down the path and smiling up into his face. 'I swear sometimes Sophie is more a child than Timothy, and I've told her over and over again not to let him climb.' She shrugged her elegant shoulders as they stopped beneath the tree. 'But she takes no notice of me.' She flicked a glance up at Sophie. 'Come down this minute.'

Seeing Sophie, her hair spiked with a few autumn leaves, tumbling free from the scarf that fought to contain the silken mass, her skirt around her thighs, didn't make Max think of her as a child—quite the opposite. She had the little boy firmly in her hold, and the two of them looked very similar, he realised. Sophie also looked childishly guilty.

'You heard what your mother said, Sophie,' Max prompted, tongue in cheek, his dark eyes glinting with amusement.

'I'm not her mother,' Margot said indignantly, and Sophie had to stifle a laugh.

Max ignored Margot and tipped his head back, his eyes taking in Sophie's lovely face and the humour twitching her lips. 'Come down this minute,' he commanded sternly, his gaze flickering over her slender body on the precarious perch, before lingering on her thighs, straddling the planks. 'Better still—hand me Timothy.' He held out his hands and glanced up, a brilliant smile slashing across his face. 'Then I will come and get you.'

His smile was so natural and so unexpected that Sophie laughed and handed Timothy into his arms. Before Tim was on his feet Sophie had swung out of the tree and was standing firmly on the ground.

Sliding a casual arm around her waist, Max pulled her into his side. 'You are a strange mixture, Sophia.' He drawled the Italian version of her name as he scanned her exquisite features. 'A beautiful, elegant woman—and yet you can act like a child.' His dark gaze held hers with compelling intensity. 'I have settled with your father—you have nothing to worry about. After seeing you with Timothy, I understand you a little better.'

Sophie very much doubted that—he thought she'd had

a host of lovers, for a start—but with his arm around her waist she felt oddly protected, and she wasn't about to argue with him.

But she *did* argue with him when her stepmother suggested they stay for dinner and the night and Max accepted.

'No—we can't possibly.' She shot Max a vitriolic look. He was seated on the sofa next to Margot in the drawing room, his long legs stretched out casually before him, looking perfectly at home, with a glass of brandy in his hand. 'I have to check on my apartment and make sure everything is okay with my neighbour.' Stiffly she rose from the armchair, and crossed the room to stare down at Max. 'If that is okay with you, Max?' she said, with a brief attempt at a smile.

It was a novel experience for Max to be looking up at Sophie. A Sophie who was actually asking his opinion instead of spitting defiance at him. For a moment he was tempted to deny her request just for devilment. But as his gaze slid appreciatively over her, and his body responded predictably, something stopped him. His tall, beautiful lover looked positively fragile. He saw the tension in her slender shoulders, the strain on her lovely face, and realised she was near breaking point.

'Yes. Of course.' He rose to his feet and read the flicker of relief in her guarded green eyes as she stepped back a little. He moved to slip a protective arm around her waist and took his cellphone from his pocket. 'I'll call the driver.' She glanced up at him and he felt her relax slightly. 'Ten minutes and we'll leave…okay?'

'Thank you,' she said softly. 'I'll just go and freshen up.'

She slipped from his hold. He watched her walk to the door, saw the effort she made to straighten her shoulders and hold her head high as Margot objected.

'Really, Sophie, we hardly ever see you. And that little apartment of yours can look after itself, for heaven's sake. You and Max *must* stay.'

He saw her head turn. 'No, I'm sorry, Margot. We must go.' She carried on out of the door, and for the first time since he had set eyes on Sophie again Max questioned what he was doing.

He looked at her so-called parents, and realised that two more self-centred people would be hard to find. He recalled Sophie telling him that her mother had died when she was eleven and she had gone to boarding school. Her father cared for her, but not enough to disrupt his lifestyle, and he was quite happy to take Max's offer to save his skin without so much as a private word with his daughter to ascertain how she really felt.

Max flicked open his cellphone and made the call, the realisation that he had behaved in just as cavalier a fashion—if not worse—making him feel as guilty as hell. Not an emotion he appreciated.

Sophie didn't go back downstairs until she saw the car arrive, and their goodbyes were mercifully brief. Her father kissed her cheek and Margot kissed air. Only Timothy was really sorry to see her go. She lifted her brother up and hugged him, smothering his little face in kisses and promising him he could come and stay with her again by the sea next summer, as he had before. She then slid into the back seat of the car.

'Are you okay?' Max asked, noting the moisture in her

eyes as he slid in beside her, after telling the driver to make for Hove.

She brushed a stray tear from her cheek, before looking bleakly at him. 'Of course. You have solved my father's problem in a day—I couldn't be happier. What do you expect me to say?' she prompted, with a negative shake of her head. And, not expecting an answer, she looked away.

Max had never seen her look more disgusted or more defeated, and unexpectedly his conscience bothered him. He had bulldozed his way into her life and into her bed without a second thought. He had taken one look at her with Abe Asamov and a red-hot tide of primitive possessiveness had blinded him to everything except a burning desire for revenge on the only woman who had ever walked out on him. But now he wasn't so sure…

'*Thank you* would be good, but not necessary.' Max caught her chin and made her face him. 'But I consider it not beyond the bounds of possibility that you might be happy with our arrangement.' He watched her green eyes widen in disbelief. 'Our sexual chemistry is great—' the slight colour rising beneath her skin encouraged him to continue '—and, contrary to the impression I might have given in the last day or two, I'm not an ogre. And with a bit of goodwill on both sides we could rub along very nicely.' Bending his dark head, he took her mouth in a quick, hard kiss. 'Think about it during the journey, while I get on with some work.' Parting his legs slightly, he lifted his briefcase to his lap, extracted the latest mining report on a new excavation in Ecuador and began to read.

Rub along very nicely—was he for real? she asked herself, her lips still tingling from his kiss. The only thing rubbing around here was his thigh against hers, with the motion of the car, and *nicely* was not an adjective she would use—*naughty*, more like. She cast a sidelong glance at his granite profile; he was so cool, so calm, so in control. How did he do that? she wondered. He was far too ruthless, too lethally male to ever be associated with the word *nice*, and she was surprised it was even in his vocabulary.

As for goodwill on both sides! She edged along the seat to put some space between them. She could just imagine how *that* would play out. An all-powerful, arrogant male like Max would consider his will good for both of them.... He certainly had so far.

Yawning, she closed her eyes. She had barely slept for two nights, and she was bone-weary and tired of thinking.

CHAPTER EIGHT

'SOPHIE...SOPHIE, wake up.' She heard the deep voice from a distance and slowly opened her eyes—to find herself with her head on Max's chest. Her arm was burrowed under his jacket and her fingers grasped the back of his shirt, while his arm was looped across her shoulders and under her other arm.

She jerked her head up. 'I fell asleep,' she murmured, stating the obvious and blushing scarlet.

'With you plastered to my chest, I did notice,' he quipped, his eyes smiling down into hers. 'But we have arrived.'

Pushing on his chest, she scrambled back to a sitting position and ran her fingers through her hair, straightening her skirt over her legs. 'I am sorry. I must have stopped you working,' she said, too embarrassed to look at him.

'Don't be. It was my pleasure,' he chuckled, and stepped out of the car.

Her apartment was on the first floor of a double-fronted detached Victorian house on a main road overlooking the beach and the sea.

'Great view,' Max remarked, glancing around as he took her hand and helped her from the car.

Standing on the pavement, it suddenly struck Sophie that she didn't want Max in her apartment. It was her private sanctuary, and when this affair was over she wanted no spectre of Max hanging around her home.

'There is no need for you to come in.' She slanted a smile at him that faded slightly as she met with intense dark eyes, studying her curiously from beneath lush black lashes. He really was incredibly attractive, and for a moment her intention wavered as she enjoyed looking at him.

She blinked rapidly and continued fighting back the blush that threatened. 'Why don't you have the driver show you around the area? He can't park here anyway, and Brighton is just along the road and very interesting,' she pointed out, with admirable cool. 'It won't take me long to pack a few things, and I have to visit my neighbour. You would be bored.' She tried to casually free her hand from his.

An ebony brow arched sardonically. 'You cannot be serious, Sophie.' In an aside he quietly dismissed the driver for the night and tightened his grip on her hand. 'I have had enough of driving around for one day.'

Sophie fitted her key into her front door lock and walked into the elegant wood-panelled foyer.

'I live on the first floor,' she murmured, and was very aware of Max's eyes on her as she walked in front of him up the enclosed staircase, and unlocked the door at the top that led into her hallway.

'Not quite up to your standards,' she said bluntly, as she led him into the sitting room. Without thought, she heeled off her shoes, dropped her bag on the usual sofa table and turned to face him. 'But I like it.'

Max gaze skimmed over her. She was bristling with defiance, and he knew she did not want him here. 'I'm sure you do,' he said smoothly, glancing around the room. 'It is charming.'

It had a sophisticated elegance, with its high ceiling and light oak floor. A grey marble fireplace housed an open fire, and a deep wide bay window that overlooked the sea was fitted with a comfortable window seat. The décor was mostly neutral, with a touch of colour in the rug and the sofas, and on one wall a waist-high long mahogany bookcase was filled with books. Above it a group of paintings were displayed.

'Would you like coffee, or a glass of wine?' Sophie asked, uncomfortable with the growing silence.

'Wine, please. Your English coffee is terrible.' Max strolled across the room and, shrugging off his jacket, draped it on the arm of the sofa and sat down.

'I left a bottle of South African chardonnay in the fridge, but I can't guarantee it will be better than the coffee,' she responded dryly.

The sight of him sprawled at ease in her home, looking as if he belonged there, confirmed Sophie's worst fears. She'd never get the image of him out of her head, she just knew it, and she was glad to escape to the kitchen-diner off the main hall.

She took off her jacket and hung it over the back of a pine chair. Taking the bottle from the fridge, she opened it and filled two large crystal glasses. She took her time, sipping a little of the wine, feeling reluctant to face him, and then realised her mistake—the quicker she got him out of here the better. She drained her glass and replaced the bottle in the fridge.

Moments later she walked back into the sitting room and placed the crystal glass on the table. 'Enjoy—the bottle is in the fridge if you want a refill. I'll just go and pack—it won't take me long. A quick call to my neighbour and we can be gone.' She knew she was babbling, but he made her nervous.

A strong hand wrapped around her wrist, and with a jerk he pulled her down beside him.

'What did you do that for?' she demanded, struggling to sit up. Another tug pulled her back, a strong arm clamping around her shoulders.

His dark eyes made a sweeping survey of her mutinous face, and he just grinned. 'Relax, Sophie; you have a lovely home—unwind and enjoy it. We are not going anywhere tonight. When you decided after lunch that you had to come here, I gave my pilot the rest of the day off—he started at ten, and he is only allowed to work twelve hours.'

His hand was warm through the fabric of her top, his thumb and fingers idly kneading her collarbone, making her achingly aware of the dangerous sensuality of his touch. Her breath caught and she had difficulty speaking for a moment. She swallowed hard, determined not to give in to his overpowering sexual attraction. She glanced at the clock on the mantelpiece. They'd left Italy at ten, and they could be back by ten if they hurried.

'It...it's just six.' She couldn't help the stammer, but carried on urgently. 'I can pack, and we can be at the airport by seven if we hurry. It is only a two and a half hour flight—we can be there by nine-thirty.'

'I'm flattered you are eager to return to my home, and your mathematical attempt on my behalf is quite impressive. Unfortunately, *cara*, you haven't allowed for continental time being an hour ahead.' Max looked at her mockingly. 'So it is not possible.'

'You can't sleep here.' Her eyes widened on his in appalled comprehension—it was her own stupid fault he was here at all. It was bad enough having him in her sitting room, but it would be a hundred times worse having him in her bedroom.

'Would you mind telling me why not?' Max enquired smoothly, his hand stroking up the side of her neck and his long fingers wrapping around her loosely tied hair.

His wide shoulders were angled towards her, and she was strikingly aware of the virile male body, the glimpse of golden skin beneath the open-necked blue shirt. She blurted out the first thing that came into her head. 'You have no clothes.'

'You are wrong. Surely you know that I am always prepared? Not that it matters—remaining naked with you will do just fine.' He grinned. 'Come on, Sophie, we both know the game is over and I won.' He tugged on her hair and tilted her head back, his glinting dark eyes capturing hers. 'Cut out the pretence. You're mine for as long as I want you—here or anywhere.'

'Only until the house is—' She tried rather futilely to deny his assumption, and was silenced by his abrupt bark of laughter.

'After meeting Nigel and Margot, I know that is never going to happen unless I make them. And I won't.'

That he had seen so easily through Margot didn't surprise her, but, forcing herself to hold his gaze, she said, 'You're probably right. But it does not alter the fact I'd rather we didn't stay here. A hotel…'

'A hotel?' His brow pleated in a frown. 'Afraid I will discover signs of your last lover in your bedroom?' His amusement vanished.

'No, of course not,' she shot back, incensed, and then wished she hadn't as his expression became strangely contemplative.

'So something else is bothering you?' His piercing black eyes narrowed shrewdly on her face and suddenly she was afraid.

'I've been away since Saturday—there is no food in the house,' she said, swiftly tearing her gaze from his, frightened he would see more in her expression than she wanted him to know.

'Is that all?' She sensed rather than saw the smile an instant before his lips brushed hers. 'I am a big man, and I need my food, but there must be a restaurant around here. We won't starve.'

Her green eyes focused on his starkly handsome face, saw his mouth curved in a sexy smile, and for a moment she was transported back in time, to the laughing, teasing Max of her youth. She felt again the heavy beat of her heart, as though it would burst from her chest, the incredible lurch in her stomach that accompanied her every sight of him, and it terrified her.

'You're right.' She forced a smile to her lips. 'Drink your wine. I need to shower and change,' she managed to say steadily. 'Climbing trees is a messy exercise.' She indicated the TV remote control on the table. 'Watch the television, if you like. I might be a while.'

Intense dark eyes skimmed over her face and lingered for a moment, then he calmly lounged back on the sofa as she rose unhindered to her feet. 'I'd rather share your shower,' he prompted softly.

'It isn't big enough,' she said without turning around and she walked slowly out of the room, closing the door behind her.

She leant against the wall, physically and emotionally drained. It had hit her like a thunderbolt when she had mentioned Saturday and made the excuse about food. Five days—it had only been five days, and her life had changed for ever. His easy dismissal of her excuse about food and her reaction had shocked her to her soul. Suddenly she realised the futility of trying to keep him out of her bedroom. It wouldn't matter where or whom she was with; the image of Max would always be in her mind.

Making herself move, she walked down the hall and into the bathroom. She stripped off her clothes and felt a chill down her spine as she realised with a sense of inevitability that she was in very real danger of becoming addicted to Max's undoubted sexual charisma all over again. She refused to call it love....

Turning on the shower, she pulled on a shower cap and stepped under the spray, her thoughts in turmoil. She had tried to dismiss her feelings for Max as a teenage crush the first time they'd been together, and had convinced herself—until last night. Now her mind was at war with her body, and the internal battle was tearing her apart. That she was Max's mistress was a huge blow to her pride, her self-respect, but the pleasure she had felt at the touch of his lips, his hands on her body, the wonder of his possession she could not deny. She could not fool herself anymore—she wanted him with a ferocity that frightened her, and he must never find out. Because if he did that would surely destroy what little self-respect she had left.

Stepping out of the shower, she dried and dressed, wondering all the time how was it possible to lust after someone when she hated the kind of man he was—and certainly didn't trust him.

Dressed in jeans and a sweater, Sophie was still asking herself the same question when, forty minutes later, she walked back into the sitting room. Max was still seated on the sofa, his briefcase open beside him and some papers in his hands. He looked up as she entered.

'Quite a transformation.'

'Not really. I always dress like this when I am at home.' She flicked a cold green glance his way. 'If there is a dress code for a mistress you should have told me.'

Max knew she was angry with him for forcing her into this situation, and in a way he didn't blame her, but on another more cynical level he didn't see what she had to complain about. She was no longer a starry-eyed virgin, not by a long way.

'Not that I am aware of. An *un*dress code, yes. Any time I say so,' he stated bluntly, his dark gaze skimming over her. She looked stunning—her long shapely legs were covered in close-fitting blue denim, and a deeper blue sweater clung to the firm thrust of her breasts. The pale blond hair was swept back into one long braid and reminded him forcibly of the teenager he had first known—and of the reason they'd parted.

He reached for her, his hands palming each side of her head, and looked deep into her angry, resentful eyes. Infuriated, he took the lush mouth with his own in a bitter, possessive kiss. If anyone had a right to be angry it was he; she had walked out on him without a second thought, at the lowest point in his life.

He felt her fingers link around his neck, the softening of her gorgeous body against his, the response she could not deny. And, disgusted with himself as much as her, he lifted his head and pushed her away. 'Where is the bathroom? I need a wash.'

As rejections went, it was a bad one, and Sophie learnt a valuable lesson. Sucking in a deep breath of air, she forced her chin up, her face expressionless. If she was to get through the next weeks or months she had to be as cool and emotionless as Max. 'First door on the right along the hall,' she replied.

Max heard the laughter as he approached the sitting room door minutes later. Light and sexy, it ripped open a Pandora's box of memories he could do without. For a moment he stood in the open door, watching her. She was sitting in the window seat, her lovely face wreathed in smiles.

'Oh, Sam, you are impossible.'

At the name Sam, Max stiffened and stepped into the room. He must have made a sound, because she turned her head towards him and the smile vanished from her face.

'Look, I can't talk now, but I promise I will try my best to get back in time. Okay?' She put the telephone down and rose to her feet.

'Sam is a friend of yours, I take it?' he prompted, and sat down on the sofa, swallowing the bitter taste that rose in his throat. How many men had sampled Sophie's luscious charms? he wondered. It was not something that had ever bothered him with his other women, and the anger surging through him felt suspiciously like jealousy.

'Yes. We spent a year backpacking together when we finished university.'

'How nice.'

Sophie glanced at him. So the word *nice* was in his vocabulary—but by the tone of his voice and the way he used it it was anything but. 'Yes, it was brilliant,' she said defiantly. Letting him know she hadn't pined for him was a good idea. 'Now, if you're ready, it is quite a pleasant night. I thought we could walk along the seafront to my favourite Italian restaurant. It is probably not in your class, but the food is great.'

'I'm relieved to hear you appreciate something about Italy,' Max grated, rising to his feet.

With him looming over her, big and threatening, she bit back the comment that sprang to mind. *It was only Max she didn't like.* Instead she said, 'If you don't mind, I'll call on my neighbour on the way out to tell her my change of plan. It won't take a moment.'

He raised an ebony brow mockingly. 'Lead on. I am in your hands.'

It was after eleven when they left the restaurant, and Sophie was feeling quite relaxed for the first time in days—though it might have had something to do with the three glasses of wine she had consumed with the meal.

Max took her hand and tucked it under his arm. 'Are you okay to walk, or shall I get a cab?'

'You should be so lucky.' She grinned up at him. 'The

pubs close at eleven—this is the rush hour for cabs. If you haven't booked one you have no chance.'

Of course he proved her wrong, by flagging one down two seconds later.

'You were right about the food—it was good. And I have never had such fast and efficient service in my life. Though I think that had more to do with your presence than mine,' Max said dryly, looping an arm around her shoulder in the back seat of the cab. 'You seem to know the family very well; you must go there a lot.'

'Oh, I do—two or three times a week when I'm at home.'

'The owner's two sons, Benito and Rocco, seem to be very friendly with you.' *Friendly* wasn't the word he really wanted to use. Fixated would be more appropriate. The two young men were clearly completely besotted with her, and, as he glanced down at her now, it wasn't hard to see why. It had been an eye-opening experience for Max.

Ironically, Max had been cross-examined by the owner as if he was Sophie's father—something Nigel Rutherford should have done earlier, but hadn't. As for the two sons, they had virtually ignored him except to shoot dagger glances at him when Sophie wasn't looking. They were much the same age as Sophie, and entirely too familiar with her for Max's liking.

'Yes, we are great pals. Sam and I met them when we were in Australia on our world travels, and they linked up with us for the last six months of our tour. We all came back to England together, and we have stayed in touch ever since.'

Dio! She had a trail of men lusting after her; they might have already had her for all he knew. 'That does not surprise me,' he snarled, his hand tightening on her shoulder at the unpalatable thought. He saw the surprise in her eyes, and with a terrific effort of will he reined in his temper. But he couldn't resist touching her, and he tilted her chin, slid a hand around the nape of her neck to hold her head.

She was a beautiful, vibrant young woman, and he had introduced her to sex—unlocked her passionate nature in what had turned out to be the most sensually exciting experience of his life, he had to admit. It was only natural she had taken other lovers after they'd parted; she wasn't cut out to be celibate.

The Abe Asamovs of this world he could deal with, but seeing her tonight, with two young men of her own peer group, so obviously relaxed and at ease with them, he'd been forcibly reminded of how much older he was than Sophie. He realised he should be thanking his lucky stars he had got her at all—she truly was priceless.

He caught her lips beneath his and explored her mouth with long, leisurely passion, before trailing a teasing path down to the beating pulse in her throat.

The cab stopping halted any further exploration, but Max kept an arm around her waist as they walked up the stairs and into her apartment. As soon as the door closed behind them he turned her in his arms.

'Your bedroom, Sophie,' he demanded, and saw the hectic flush of arousal in her face. He nipped playfully on her lower lip. 'Quickly would be good, *cara*.'

He stared down at her and, held against his big, taut body, Sophie realised that what was to follow was as inevitable as night following day. With every cell in her body crying out for what he was offering—why fight it? And, easing out of his arms, she reached for his hand and linked her fingers with his, leading him along the hall to the door opposite the sitting room and opening it.

Max laughed out loud, a rich, dark sound in the stillness of the utterly feminine room. The carpet was a soft ivory, and along the wall furthest from the door was a four-poster bed, draped in yards and yards of white muslin tied with pink satin bows. A delicate dresser and matching wardrobes in antique white, delicately painted with roses, plus a matching chaise longue were arranged around the other walls. But it was the big bay window that amused him.

'How on earth do you sleep with all those eyes watching you?' The window seat was lined with a startling array of dolls in every form of dress, and on the floor in the bay was a Georgian-style dolls' house.

'Very well, as it happens,' Sophie declared, abruptly recovering from the sensual daze he had evoked in her. Pulling her hand from his, she said, 'And what has it got to do with you, anyway?' He was never going to come here again, if she could help it.

Dark eyes glinting with amusement sought hers, and a predatory smile revealed brilliant white teeth. 'I'm intrigued as to why a woman of your intelligence and sophistication would have a bedroom like this.'

'The dolls' house was my mother's, and as for the dolls—some I have had for years, and I've got into the habit of collecting others from every country I visit,' she said defensively. 'I do have another bedroom you can use. I'll show you.' She grasped the chance and turned to leave.

But he stopped her, his arm snaking around her waist to keep her clamped against him.

'No, Sophie, this will do just fine,' he informed her softly, and he bent his head just enough to brush his lips against her own.

She jerked her head back in rejection. 'In Venice you have your own bedroom. At least let me keep the same distinction in *my* home,' she demanded.

'Remember our deal—sex anywhere, any time, my choice,' he drawled, and he caught her mouth again and this time didn't stop.

Helplessly her eyelids fluttered down, and she raised her slender arms to wrap them around his shoulders, her body arching into his. Her tongue traced the roof of his mouth and curled with his, her blood flowing like liquid heat in her veins. His hands were all over her; his long fingers finding the snap of her jeans and sweeping up her spine under her sweater to open her bra, then sweeping around to find the thrusting swell of her breasts.

Her hand darted down to tear at his shirt, and she whimpered when his mouth left hers. Her eyes still closed, her slender body shaking with need, he lifted her onto the frilly white coverlet and with a deftness that underlined his experience she was soon naked.

At the touch of cool air on her skin her eyes opened, and her gaze fixed on the masculine perfection of Max standing by the bed. Big and formidable, his muscular, hair-roughened chest was rising not quite steadily, and his lean hips and hard thighs framed the great dynamic power of his sex.

How often had she lain in this bed with the image of a

naked Max haunting her dreams? The erotic fantasies she had built in her mind of him appearing and declaring his undying love while she drove him mad with desire had left her sleepless and frustrated.

'Max,' she murmured throatily, her fantasy now a reality, and her green eyes darkened as with a slow, seductive smile she lifted her arms to him.

He chuckled a deep, sexy sound that vibrated across her nerve-endings and, leaning over her, curved his hand around her throat. He looked deep into her eyes. 'Yes, Sophie—say my name.'

His hand slid down over her breast and her stomach to settle between her legs. He held her gaze as a finger slipped between the soft folds and stroked once, twice, and she shuddered, groaned out her frustration when he stopped. Then he was beside her on the bed, his dark head dropping, his mouth taking the groan from her throat as his tongue stroked hers in a wicked dance of desire.

Lost between fantasy and reality, Sophie reached for him, her slender hand curving eagerly around his neck and raking into the silken hair of his head. Her other hand stroked down over his broad chest, her subtle fingers grazing a pebble-like nipple on their descent down his sleek, muscled body to his flat belly. She touched him where she had never touched him before, her hand closing around the long, hard length of his erection, a finger stroking the velvet tip. She felt his great body jerk in response, heard his groan and gloried in it as her hand moved inquisitively down to the root of his male essence. Then abruptly he caught her straying hands and, rearing back, placed them on either side of her body.

'Now you want to play?' he growled, his dark gaze sweeping over her body, lingering on the perfect rose-tipped breasts, and lower, to the soft blond curls at the apex of her thighs, then dropping to her spectacular long legs and moving back to her face. '*Dio*, you are exquisite.'

His compliment fed her fantasy as his avid glance seared her flesh. Sophie was on fire for him, liquid heat pooling between her thighs. She reached for him again, her hands stroking over his wide shoulders.

He looked down at her, his sultry smile a sensual promise, and parted her thighs to move between them. He took her mouth once more in a fiercely passionate kiss, his hand cupping her where she wanted him, his long fingers easing again between the sensitive folds.

She clung to him, the tantalising movement of his clever fingers driving her wild with want, and when his mouth dipped lower, to draw on her straining nipples, she cried out. 'Please, Max, please,' her whole body quivering with need.

At her cry, Max groaned hoarsely and lifted his head. Her green eyes glazed with passion, she was *so* wet and *so* ready. Lifting her hips, his great body taut with strain, his breathing harsh, he plunged into her. She was tight and hot, and, using all his skill and self-control, he moved— sometimes with shallow strokes, and then more intensely, with long, full strokes ever deeper. He wanted to make this last. He wanted to blot out every other lover from her mind.

Sophie had never known such almost painful pleasure existed as he swept her along in an ever-increasing fero-cious tidal wave of tense, torturous desire.

Max rolled onto his back and lifted her above him, his

strong hands firm on her waist, crazy with need as she hovered on the brink and stared down into his dark face. He was watching her with a feral light in his night-black eyes, and he stilled for a second whilst she rushed headlong towards her climax. She cried out at the tug of his mouth on her rigid nipples, and at the same time the power of him filling her to the hilt with ever more powerful strokes sent her over the edge into a delirious climax. She was wanton in her ecstasy, pushing down hard on him with every increasing spasm. She felt his great body buck and shudder, and he called her name once in a voice that was close to pain as he joined her in a cosmic explosion of raw, passionate release that was completely beyond their control.

Sophie collapsed on top of him, breathless and shaking, burying her head in the soft curls of his broad chest. She had never known such intense sensations were possible. For a few blissful moments while she lay in the circle of her arms she could almost believe it was love: the familiar scent of him, the weight of him, the pounding of their hearts almost in unison. Then he moved her over onto her back and flopped down beside her, and the fantasy vanished as the silence lengthened.

Suddenly she felt cold; there was no love, only a primitive lust. Of course it was great…Max was an expert at sex, and so he should be…he'd had plenty of practice, by all accounts, she reminded herself. She clenched her fists at her sides, to prevent her weaker self reaching for him again.

The movement of the mattress told her he had stood up, but she didn't look; she couldn't, in case he saw the hurt in her eyes. She heard the door open, and moved to slip beneath the covers, a shiver of revulsion assailing her at what he had made her. A willing slave to her sexuality, nothing more....

She pulled the lace-covered duvet up around her chin and buried her head in the pillow. She heard the door close, and then nothing.... He had probably found the spare bedroom. It was no more than she expected, and she had to learn to live with it....

'Sophie.' He drawled her name softly and she turned, her eyes widening in surprise. He was standing by the bed stark naked, with two wine glasses in one hand and the half-full bottle of wine in the other.

'A nightcap? Or perhaps a drink before the second round?' he prompted with a wicked grin. And she couldn't help it—she grinned back.

Sophie yawned and opened her eyes. She blinked at the sunlight streaming through the window, and then blinked again as a dark head blotted out the sun.

'Max,' she murmured, and she was intensely aware of his long body against her own. 'You stayed all night.'

'I had nowhere else to go.' He dropped a swift kiss on her softly parted lips. 'Unfortunately I do now.' His hand curved around to cup her breast and she sighed. 'I know,' he said, and his thumb grazed her rosy nipple. 'Unfortunately we haven't any time. My pilot has a take-off slot in eighty minutes.' Withdrawing his hand, he rolled off the bed. 'Come on—the car will be here any moment now.'

Twenty minutes later, washed and dressed in a short red and black kilt-style skirt, with a soft black mohair sweater pulled hastily over her head and her feet pushed into red pumps, Sophie slid into the limousine.

She was still trying to make sense of this new, relaxed Max when they boarded his jet and a steward served breakfast.

CHAPTER NINE

DIEGO WAS WAITING with the launch as they exited the airport at noon, and their return to the *palazzo* was swift. Entering the elegant hall, Sophie was shocked to see a group of six smiling adults lined up to meet them. She was surprised to discover as Max made the introductions that Diego did not run the house on his own. Maria, his wife, was the cook, Tessa, their married daughter, was the maid and her husband Luke was the gardener…quite the family affair.

'I didn't know you had a garden,' Sophie said as the staff dispersed.

'Obviously you need a tour. Diego will take your luggage upstairs while I show you around.' Max waved around the ground floor. 'Dining room, study and morning room and grand salon. Beneath is the kitchen, utility room and Diego's apartment, and beneath that the cellars.'

Of course—the massive steps to the entrance concealed the fact this was actually the first floor, and not the ground, she realised as he led her around the back of the staircase and opened a large double door. To her surprise inside there was a fully equipped games room and gym, with a swimming pool half in and half out of the house. The exterior part had glass walls and a roof that opened to the sky. Steps led down into a walled garden.

'Feel free to use this whenever you like.' Striding back to the reception hall, he added, 'I have some work to catch up on, so I will leave you to your own devices—but remember lunch is at one-thirty.'

She saluted. 'Yes, oh master.' But he was not amused. The Max of last night, who'd drunk wine in her bed, was gone, and the autocratic tyrant was back.

'That is exactly what I am, and don't you forget,' he replied stiffly, and without another word disappeared into his study.

Sophie made her way upstairs to her bedroom just as the young maid Tessa was disappearing through the open door of the dressing room with the smallest case in her hand. 'No—please, I can unpack myself,' Sophie said with a smile. From what she had seen so far there was precious little else for her to do around here—except await her master's bidding.

But she was too late. After Tessa had left she occupied her time by placing a few personal items—her make-up, jewellery box and perfume—on the small, ornate antique dressing table. It was just for show, however, because she had no intention of using the dressing room for anything other than storing clothes now that she knew she shared it with Max. And at that moment he appeared.

'I forgot to give you these,' he said as he walked towards her. Stopping at her side, he dropped something on the dressing table. 'I have opened an Italian bank account for you, as agreed, and that is your credit card.' He glanced at her. 'After lunch we are going out, and much as I like that short, flirty skirt I don't want you wearing it in public. Get changed.' And, swinging on his heel, he left as abruptly as he had arrived.

What did he *want* her to wear? Sackcloth and ashes? Sophie fumed as she stripped off and headed for the shower. She had lived on her own and been her own boss for years. Kowtowing to a man was not in her nature—especially not to an arrogant, ruthless man like Max.

She frowned as she stood under the soothing spray. Sophie knew herself well. She was not cut out to be a mistress; she was far too independent. But the trouble was, until her father's business was secure she had no choice.

Deep in thought, she walked back out of the bathroom and into the dressing room. What she needed was a strategy for living with Max that would not leave her an emotional wreck when they parted. Inexperienced as she was, she knew Max was right: they *were* sexually compatible, dangerously so, and it would be very easy for her to become addicted to the man. She had to guard against that at all costs.

Slipping into white briefs and a matching bra, she opened the wardrobe door, her hand reaching for a pair of denim jeans, and stopped. She wasn't at home; this *palazzo* would never be her home. Max had told her that a mistress agreed with her man at all times, and an inkling of an idea occurred to her.

She entered the dining room half an hour later, dressed in a sage-green double-breasted jacket with only a bra beneath, and a matching slim-fitting skirt that ended just above her knees. She had scraped two swathes of hair back and fastened them in a loop at the back of her head. The rest she had left loose, to fall down her back. Her make-up was perfect, but a lot more than she would usually use, and on her feet she was wearing three-inch-heeled stilettos.

Max was standing by the drinks trolley, a glass in his hand, and turned as she walked in. His hard, dark eyes swept slowly over her from head to toe, lingering on the plunging V of her jacket and even longer on her legs. He was examining her like some a master in a slave market. She could feel angry colour rising in her cheeks, but she fought it down.

'You have taken my advice, I see. Would you like a drink?'

'Yes, please.' Her temper rising at his arrogant certainty that she would do as she was told, she had almost said no. But, mindful of the part she had decided to play as she had dressed, she agreed. Hadn't Max told her a mistress always said yes? The beginnings of a smile twitched her lips. This might even be fun.

'Do you always eat in here?' she asked, and smiled up at him as she took the glass of wine he offered her. It was a large, elegant room, but her preference would be to eat somewhere less formal.

'Yes, when I am here. Which is not that often.'

'Well, if you don't mind, when I am on my own would it be all right for me to eat somewhere smaller—the kitchen, perhaps?' she asked.

'If you like.' Max pulled out her chair for her as Diego entered with the first course, then took his own seat.

As the meal progressed Max grew puzzled. Sophie had changed from the tiny skirt into an elegant suit, as he had suggested, but it did not help him much. Because although her legs were halfway covered, he could see her cleavage—and he was pretty sure she wore nothing under the jacket. She had left her gorgeous hair loose, and she was smiling and talking perfectly politely, agreeing to everything he said. So why did he get the feeling something was wrong?

'So, where are you taking me this afternoon?' Sophie asked as she took a sip of coffee, the meal over.

Max knew where he wanted to take her—straight to bed. But he reined in his baser impulse; there was something different about her and it infuriated him because he could not pinpoint the change. 'I am taking you to the jewellers to fulfil my side of the bargain,' he said, shoving back his chair and standing up. 'I promised you diamonds instead of crystal.'

'Oh, yes. I forgot.' Sophie stood up as well. She didn't want his damn diamonds, but in her new role she had to agree. 'But there is no hurry,' she couldn't help adding.

'I'm a busy man, and I am never usually here on a Friday. As I am here, I want to get the matter settled now.'

Sophie bit down hard on her bottom lip. 'Yes, of course,' she replied and headed for the door before she lost her cool and landed him a slap in the face. He was talking to her as if she was some blond bimbo. But then that was what he *thought* she was....

'Sophie?' Her skin prickled at the way he drawled her name, and a long arm slipped around her waist, halting her progress. 'We don't *have* to go out....'

She glanced up at him, saw the intention in his dark eyes. The warmth of his arm around her waist was making her temperature rise—and with it her temper.

'Yes, we do,' she said sweetly, and her plan to say *yes* to everything suddenly seemed very easy.

Half an hour later, when they walked into the jewellers, it was not quite so easy. The jeweller saw them seated and then presented a staggering array of diamond necklaces, earrings and bracelets for their perusal.

'Do you like this set?' Max indicated a stunning waterfall of diamonds.

'Yes,' she said, and continued to say yes to everything he suggested.

'Oh, for heaven's sake, chose one,' Max snarled, finally losing his patience, and he saw her luscious lips curve in a secretive smile.

She turned wide, innocent green eyes up to him. 'You choose, Max. After all, you are paying for it so it has to please you.'

Then it hit him. The little witch had been saying yes to everything, agreeing with everything he said, since the moment she'd come down to lunch. It was every man's fantasy to have a lover who said yes to everything, so why did it feel so damn irritating?

Indicating the waterfall set, he bought and paid for it, ignoring Sophie, and then, taking her arm, he pulled her to her feet and they left the shop.

'I am on to you, lady,' he drawled, turning her into his arms, his dark eyes gleaming down into hers. 'Will you jump into the canal for me, Sophie?' He felt her stiffen in his arms. 'Or kiss me, here and now?' And he saw the guilt in her green eyes. She knew she had been found out. God, she was a stubborn creature—but beautiful with it. He made it easy for her. 'Say yes to the latter. You know you have to,' he chuckled.

The broad grin and the laughter in his eyes were Sophie's undoing. 'Yes,' she laughed, and he bent his head, taking advantage of her open mouth to slip his tongue between her parted lips. Her hands slipped up around his neck—and that was how Gina found them.

'Max? Max—what on earth are you doing?'

Max lifted his head but kept an arm around Sophie's waist. 'Gina.' He grinned. 'You're a doctor—and you don't know?' He felt the sudden tension in Sophie and tightened his grip. She had to face his sister some time—the one witness to her brutal dismissal of him years ago. 'I didn't know you had stayed in Venice.'

'Even doctors are entitled to a holiday. But I am surprised *you* are still here. Though I can see why,' she said drolly, with the lift of a delicate brow in Sophie's direction.

Sophie looked at the small dark woman and her companion, another slightly older woman, and wished the ground would open up and swallow her whole. To be caught kissing in broad daylight was bad enough, but to be caught by Gina, his ex-lover—or maybe not ex—was doubly embarrassing.

'You know Sophie, of course,' Max said suavely, and glanced down at her. 'And you remember Gina, *cara*?'

As if she could forget. 'Yes,' she said slowly, and gave Gina a polite smile. 'Nice to see you again.' Why on earth had she said that? She couldn't give a damn if she never saw either her or Max ever again.

'Nice to see you, too,' Gina agreed. 'This is my friend Rosa.' She made the introduction. 'We thought we would do some shopping, then stop for a coffee at Florian. What are you and Max up to?'

'The same.' Max answered for her. 'Except we have finished our shopping.'

'My God, Sophie, I don't believe it—you actually got the world's worst chauvinist to take you shopping!' Gina laughed. 'If you hang around longer this time he might even become halfway human.'

Confused by Gina's obviously genuine laughter, and the lack of malice in her tone, Sophie gave a wry smile. 'I doubt it.'

A husky chuckle greeted her words and Max glanced at his stepsister. 'Watch it, Gina. I don't want you frightening Sophie off with your biased view of me.' He drew Sophie closer to his side.

'So it would seem,' Gina said, slanting an amused look at the pair of them. 'It is to be hoped—'

'Are we going for coffee or what?' Rosa intervened. 'I need my caffeine fix.'

'Yes—sure. Why don't you and Sophie join us, Max?' Gina asked.

An hour later, when they left the coffee shop, Sophie was none the wiser about Max and Gina's real relationship. On the launch going back to the house she replayed the meeting in her mind. Surprisingly, the conversation had been easy. Rosa, she had discovered, was married with two boys—who sounded like holy terrors from the anecdotes she had shared with them. It was obvious Max and Gina were close, and totally at ease with each other, but whether it was sexual Sophie didn't know. She had sensed under their apparently friendly conversation and laughter a kind of tension—and it wasn't just the tension *she* always felt around Max. It was something more, but she couldn't put her finger on it.

'Rosa was funny—and Gina was quite pleasant,' she said slowly as they entered the house.

'Were you surprised?' Max asked with a sardonic lift of an ebony brow. 'You shouldn't be—she almost always is.'

'Yes, if you say so,' she murmured.

With his finger and thumb he tilted her chin. 'Have I missed something?' he demanded. His dark eyes narrowed intently on her upturned face. 'Or are we back to the yes game again, I wonder?' His astute gazed dropped to the lush curve of her mouth and his hand tightened slightly.

She knew his intention, felt it in the sudden tension between them.

'No to both,' she said hurriedly, and lowered her lashes to mask her own reaction.

'You look tired. Have a rest before dinner.'

'I know your kind of rest,' she said with biting sarcasm, and, shrugging off his hand, she headed for the stairs.

But she didn't escape completely.

She was standing in front of the dressing table, having kicked off her shoes and shrugged off her jacket, and was about to remove her make-up when Max walked in.

'You forgot this.' He strolled over and dropped the jewellers box on the table, his cold dark eyes meeting hers in the mirror. 'The deal is finalised. I always keep my word— just make sure you keep yours.'

Over breakfast the next morning Sophie could barely look at him. He had come to her bed last night and made her wear the diamonds while he made love to her—no, *had sex* with her. And she had never felt so demeaned in her life.

'I am going to the family estate this morning,' he informed her coldly, rising from the table. 'Since the death of my father I need to help out with the running of the Quintano hotels. I'll be back Sunday night. In the meantime, if you want to go out you are not to go alone. Diego will accompany you at all times—understood?'

It was a very different Sophie who, six weeks later, looked in the same dressing table mirror and slipped a diamond drop earring into her earlobe. They were going to a charity dinner, and she could hear Max moving around in the dressing room. He had returned an hour earlier, from a week-long trip to Ecuador, and they were in danger of being late because he had joined her in the shower....

Max was an incredible and determined lover, and she had long since given up on trying to resist him. He was also very generous—her lips twisted at her reflection in the glass. The Versace emerald-green evening gown revealed more than it concealed, a pair of designer green satin shoes were on her feet, and the large diamond Van Cleef earrings with matching necklace completed the look. Yes—she looked what she was: a rich man's mistress.

In bed, she had no defence, and only a strong sense of self-protection stopped her revealing her ever-deepening feelings for Max. But paradoxically her image in the mirror satisfied her, because it made it easier to play the part of a cool sophisticate around him.

Surprisingly, it seemed to work, and they did—to use

Max's words—*rub along* quite well. Every night he was in Venice he came to her bed and aroused her with a slow, deliberate eroticism, aware of every nuance of her response until she cried out for release and he tipped her over the edge into ecstasy. Sometimes he came with her, and sometimes he followed her. Either way, they ended up breathless and spent—but also silent. Sophie didn't dare speak, and she guessed Max had no reason to; he had got what he wanted. As often as not he stayed till the morning and they made love again. And sometimes when she was locked in his embrace she almost believed it was love instead of lust....

Over the weeks she had developed her own routine to make life bearable, and the kitchen had become her favourite room in the house. She got along well with Maria, Tessa and her three children, and she took great pleasure in teaching the young ones English—the adults benefited as well.

She had quickly realised Max worked incredibly long hours. Sometimes he was here, in his study, but he was just as likely to fly halfway around the world for a couple of days. When he was at home he spent at least two or three days a week—always including Friday—at his head office in Rome.

Sophie had travelled to Rome with him only once, about a month ago. He had worked all day, taken her shopping in the evening, then to dinner in an intimate little restaurant, and finally to bed in his penthouse apartment. She had thoroughly enjoyed the experience; somehow in Rome she had not felt like a mistress.

But the following morning, after Max had left for the office she had again. She'd taken a shower and, looking in the bathroom cabinet, hoping to find a toothbrush, had discovered a bottle of perfume and various other female toiletries—plus a large black hairslide and a bottle of prescription medicine in Gina's name. The slide she knew could *not* be Gina's—the woman had close-cut hair.

The next time Max asked her to accompany him to Rome she refused, with the excuse that it was the wrong time of the month.

Sophie frowned now, as she clipped on the other earring. He had dismissed her excuse as irrelevant—saying there were many routes to sexual pleasure—and it had only been when she'd insisted she felt ill that he had given in. She had seen in his sardonic smile as he'd said, 'Have it your way,' that he didn't believe her.

Sophie knew from Maria that she was the only woman Max had brought to live in the *palazzo*. To the romantic but conservative Maria that meant they would marry, and Sophie didn't like to disillusion her. Sophie now accepted that Max shared her bed—honesty forced her to admit she couldn't resist him—but she couldn't accept sharing his bed in Rome. Not when he had all his other lovers.

Sophie spent quite a lot of time on her own. Max, she presumed, continued to go and visit the family estate—though he had never told her so since that first time—or perhaps he stayed in Rome. The fact that he never asked her to accompany him again didn't bother her. At least that was what she told herself. And when he telephoned her occasionally she never asked him where he was; she was afraid to show too much interest.

She enjoyed the freedom to explore Venice—not that she was entirely free; Diego had strict instructions to accompany her when she went out. But, on the upside, Diego was a fount of information. She had visited St Mark's and sat outside the Café Florian, sipping coffee and watching the world go by. They had visited the Guggenheim and the Accademia, and many more smaller art galleries, which she would never have known existed without Diego, plus countless churches filled with stunning masterpieces that one would not normally expect to see outside a museum.

The city itself was probably the most beautiful and romantic in the world—but how much better it would have been to explore the tiny alleys and hidden *piazzas,* to linger in the small cafés with someone she loved, she thought sadly. Someone like Max....

If she was honest she missed him when he was away— she kept telling herself she hated him and it was just sex, but it was becoming harder and harder to do. He occupied her thoughts all the time. Like now, she realised, her forehead pleating in a frown.

'Why the frown?' a deep, dark voice drawled.

Sophie turned her head to see that Max had emerged from the dressing room and was watching her with a look of genuine concern in his eyes. Her heart squeezed in her chest. He had his dinner jacket in one hand and was wearing black trousers and a white evening shirt that contrasted brilliantly with his tanned complexion. He looked staggeringly attractive. But then he always did to her. And it was in that moment she knew she loved him. She could fool herself no longer. She loved him, probably always had and always would, and the knowledge terrified her.

Sophie looked back at her reflection in the mirror, to give herself time to get over the shock of realising how she truly felt about Max and to try and compose herself. 'I was wondering if these earrings were too much,' she finally answered, turning back to him with her face a sophisticated calm mask—she hoped.

'Not a bit—you look exquisite,' he declared, dropping his jacket on the bed. His gaze swept appreciatively over her. A slight smile quirked the corners of his sensual mouth and she saw the gleam of gold in his dark eyes and recognised that look. Given it was no more than half an hour since they had indulged, and given the scary knowledge that she loved him, she resented the ease with which he aroused an answering response in her own body.

She lifted her chin—an angry sparkle in her green eyes. 'You paid for it,' she snapped, and his eyes narrowed fractionally at her sudden outburst.

'True,' Max said, and stepped towards her. 'I also pay for your services.' He stretched out his arm.

'We haven't time,' she gasped, taking a step back.

'Oh, Sophie, you really do have a one-track mind—not that I am complaining,' he mocked. And, grasping her hand, he dropped a platinum cufflink in her palm. 'Fasten this for me.' He shook his outstretched arm, amusement dancing in his dark eyes. 'I can never manage the right as easily as the left.'

Her lips twitched. 'You, Max Quintano, can and do manage *everything*,' she said, but fixed the cufflink, admiring the fine dark hair on his wrist as she did so.

'And that is what irks you, my beauty.' Slipping an arm around her bare shoulders, he brought her into close contact with his hard body. His mouth closed over hers in a long deep kiss. 'How about we skip this party and stay here? I have been away too long, and I have not had nearly enough of you yet.'

'You're actually asking my opinion?' she prompted, with the delicate arch of a fine brow. 'Now, that *is* a first. You usually do as you like.'

'True,' he said, all arrogant virile male, his hand sliding down over her bottom. 'But you also like.' He smiled as he felt her shiver.

'Maybe.' She recognised the sensual amusement in his dark gaze. 'But you're crazy if you think I got all dressed up like this just for you to undress me.'

'Crazy about you—yes,' he said, with a wry smile that completely stunned her. It was the closest he had ever got to hinting that he cared, and a tiny seed of hope lodged in her heart. He moved his hand to curve it around her waist and added, 'But I promised to attend this charity dinner, so the undressing will have to wait until we return.' He ushered her towards the door. 'Though maybe we can fool around in the launch on the way. What do you think?' he asked, with roguish lift of his black eyebrows.

He looked like a swashbuckling pirate, Sophie thought, and, shaking her head, she laughed. She couldn't help it. At moments like this she could almost believe they were a happy normal couple.

The dinner-dance was a select affair held at Hotel Cypriani, and with Max's hand linked in hers she walked into the elegant room. The first person she saw was Gina, in a group of half a dozen distinguished-looking people. She turned her head and laughed at something that had been said, then caught sight of Max and came rushing over.

'Max, *caro*.' She grabbed his arm and stood on tiptoe,

her body pressed against his side, to give him a kiss full on his lips. Still clinging to his arm, she turned to Sophie.

'Sophie, I'm surprised to see *you* here. I didn't think this was your thing. But we do need all the support we can get,' she said with a smile, and turned back to Max. 'It's weeks since I've seen you. I am so glad you could make it.'

Gina could not have made it plainer that it was Max who interested her and she only tolerated Sophie's presence at his side, Sophie thought, her new-found love making her hypersensitive as jealousy, swift and painful, sliced through her. When had the conventional public kiss on both cheeks developed to a full-blown kiss on the mouth?

Then, out of the blue, a distant memory hit her like a punch in the stomach. Old Man Quintano had strongly disapproved of Max and Gina's relationship, but now he was dead there was no one to object to them marrying.

Suddenly Max's desire to have her as his mistress made more sense, and the blood turned to ice in her veins as the reality of the situation sank in. Max was a highly sexed man—as Sophie knew all too well. One woman would probably never be enough for him. As a teenager *she* had been the prospective bride, because she might be pregnant, and Gina the lover; now the situation was reversed, and *she* was cast in that role.

'You're right—this isn't my thing.' And Sophie didn't mean the dinner. She meant Max and Gina's relationship. 'In fact, I will quite happily leave.' Sophie saw no reason to pretend any more. A ménage à trois had never been and never would be for her, and she tried to pull her hand from Max's.

Max's jaw tightened in anger. Enjoying Sophie's exquisite body, he had almost dismissed the reason she had left him, excusing her behaviour by telling himself that she had been young and naturally frightened of the prospect of tying herself to a sick man. Now he knew better—she didn't give a damn about anything but her own pleasure. What kind of man did that make him? Lusting after a heartless woman who had quite happily been Abe Asamov's mistress and heaven knew how many more?

He gave her a hard look, saw the beautiful, expression-less face and the cold green eyes, and said with chilling emphasis, 'This is Gina's night—her cancer charity.' He smiled coldly and twisted Sophie's hand around her back to pull her against him in what looked like a loving gesture. 'You will stay and be civil to everyone,' he murmured against her ear. 'You will act the part of my loving con-sort—something I know you are good at. After all, that *is* what I pay you for,' he reminded her with sibilant softness. He felt her tense, and simply tightened his grip.

Then he turned his attention to Gina. 'I am sure your night is going to be a great success. Don't mind Sophie. She did not mean to offend you. Did you, *cara*?' His hard black eyes turned on her.

'No, it was a joke,' Sophie said feebly. But the joke was on her. She had finally recognised in her heart and mind that she loved Max, only to find out half an hour later nothing had changed.

Sophie sank into the seat Max held out for her, glad to be finally free of his restraining hold. But it was only in memory of her mother that she sat down at all. She was sick to her stomach and simmering with anger. From the teasing lover of an hour ago, he was once more the ruthless, autocratic swine who had forced her to be his mistress. She hadn't missed the threat in his words, and he couldn't have spelt out more clearly exactly where his loyalty lay. And with that knowledge the faint seed of hope she had nurtured earlier of something more than sex between them died a bitter death.

She straightened the slim-fitting skirt of her gown over her thighs, fighting to retain her composure, and when she did lift her head her lips twisted cynically as she noted the seating arrangement. Gina was seated on Max's left and she was seated on his right—now, why didn't that surprise her?

She forced a smile to her lips as introductions were made all round, and realised they were mostly medical professionals. She accepted the wine offered and did her best to ignore Max. It wasn't hard, as Gina engaged him in conversation—for which Sophie was truly grateful.

As course followed course and the wine flowed, the conversation became more animated. But Sophie took very little part. These people were probably all very good and clever, but she was in no mood for talking.

Beside her, Max wore the mantle of dominant and sophisticated male with ease, his input into the conversation witty and astute. His occasional comments to Sophie were smoothly made with a smile, and to any onlooker he appeared a caring partner, with a touch on her arm, an offer to fill her glass. Only she could see the restrained anger in his gaze, and it took all her will-power simply to respond to him civilly. The way she felt right now, she couldn't care less if she never spoke to him again.

She'd got over him once and she would again, Sophie

vowed. But although she tried to ignore it, the pain in her heart refused to go away.

For the rest of the meal she avoided his glance, with her head bent down, concentrating on her food, although she had never felt less like eating in her life.

It was when coffee was served that the conversation really became boisterous. Sophie gathered the discussion was about ways of raising money for cancer research and involving patients at the same time. But she wasn't paying much attention; it was taking every atom of self-control she possessed simply to stay seated at the table with Gina and Max. Her mind was reeling at the thought of them together—and heaven knew how many other women had shared the pleasure of his sexual expertise.

'Why not have an auction, with the beautiful Sophie selling kisses?' a voice declared loudly, and at the sound of her name Sophie raised her head. A man sitting opposite her, whom she had noticed earlier staring at her cleavage and ignored, was ogling her again. 'The patients could buy them as well. I know if I was seriously ill a kiss from a gorgeous woman would do me good.' Everyone laughed, and all eyes were on her.

'That would never work.' Gina chuckled. 'Sophie is a beautiful, decorative woman, but not cut out to visit the sick. She'd probably give them a heart attack. Isn't that right, Sophie?' Gina quipped, and everyone laughed.

It was a hurtful thing to say, and for a moment Sophie was struck dumb. Gina knew nothing at all about her—and yet she felt able to pass comment on her. She glanced around the table; nobody here really knew her, she thought, so why bother to argue?

'If you say so,' she murmured.

'I wouldn't allow her to anyway,' Max drawled, and reached for her hand.

But she avoided his hand *and* his glittering gaze by picking up her glass and draining it before she put it back down. She wished she was anywhere in the world but here.

A veined hand patted hers on the table. 'It was just a joke. We medical people *en masse* tend to lose our sensitivity a little—don't take it to heart.' It was the professor seated next to her who spoke, quietly seeing what no one else had noticed.

Sophie was touched and grateful for his intervention, as it allowed her to turn her back on Max and look up with moisture-filled eyes into the old man's face.

'Thank you,' she said, trying to smile. 'But it is an emotive subject for me,' she explained quietly. 'My mother died of breast cancer when I was eleven. For two years before that I did my best to nurse her, but I was still a child and obviously not up to these people's standards.' She attempted to joke.

'Forget it, and do me the honour of this dance.' The professor stood up. 'If you do not mind, Signor Quintano?' he asked Max over the top of Sophie's head.

Max glanced at him, and sharply at Sophie. Her body was angled towards the professor, all her attention on the older man. The witch had the nerve to ignore him and then captivate the eminent Professor Manta, right before his eyes. The old fool was grinning all over his face as if he had discovered the cure for cancer. How the hell did she do it?

'Be my guest.' He couldn't do much else with Gina tugging on his arm again. Since when had his sister become such a chatty type? he wondered in exasperation as he watched Sophie and the professor take to the dance floor.

'Feel better now?' the professor asked Sophie, his brown eyes twinkling into hers.

'Yes—yes, I do.' She relaxed in his formal hold. 'I am not usually so emotional, but the comment about me not being cut out to visit the sick caught me on the raw and I didn't see the joke. You see, the anniversary of my mother's death was the twenty-fifth of November—three days ago.' And also she had realised she loved a man who didn't deserve to be loved.

'You are a lovely, emotional little woman—and that is nothing to be ashamed of,' he reassured her gently.

Sophie did smile at that. 'Hardly little.'

'Maybe not, but you are extremely feminine. Something, I am afraid, that in my experience can sometimes get knocked out of female doctors over the years.'

'Feminine I like,' she chuckled, appreciating the distinguished-looking man more by the minute—even if he was a bit of a chauvinist.

'Good. Now, a change of subject is called for, so tell me about you. Are you on holiday here? And what do you normally do when not visiting our fair city?'

Whether he knew of her connection with Max or not she didn't care. Because she instinctively knew the professor was a gentleman.

'I am visiting a friend for a while, but I'm a linguist and I work as a translator. Sometimes I teach, but at the minute all I do is teach English to the cook's grandchildren.'

With his next words, much to Sophie's surprise, Professor Manta was offering her a job. Apparently he was on the board of governors at the private school that his grandchildren attended, and they were looking for a language teacher—someone to fill in for the rest of the term, as the present teacher was on extended sick leave.

'I'm flattered, though I'm not sure it will be possible,' she said, but she took the card the professor offered and promised to ring him tomorrow, to let him know one way or the other.

Max couldn't believe it. He saw her take the card from the old goat as they approached the table and he had had enough. He rose to his feet and, with a stiff smile for the grinning professor, wrapped his arm tightly around Sophie's waist.

'It is time we left now.'

Sophie felt his proprietorial arm around her and tensed, but refused to look at him. Instead she said good night to the professor, and a general good night to the rest of the company. Gina she ignored. But Max's prolonged goodbye to his stepsister more than made up for Sophie's lapse in manners.

CHAPTER TEN

'YOU are very quiet, *cara.*' He dipped his head towards her as they exited the room. 'Upset that I took you away from your latest conquest?'

His words were soft, but she heard the angry edge in his tone, and when she tilted her head back she saw his eyes glittering hard as jet.

'The professor is not a conquest but a gentleman,' she snapped. 'Something you would know nothing about.'

'Maybe not,' he said, his smile cruel. 'But I *do* know you're no lady. The fact is you are available to the highest bidder, and at the moment it happens to be me. So hand over the card he gave you—he is not for you.'

'God! Your mind never lifts above the gutter!'

She stared at him. His face was a mask of barely contained anger, and for a fleeting moment she wondered if he was jealous. No…for that he would have to care, and all he cared about was getting his money's worth. He had just said so.

'It just so happens that Professor Manta offered me a job. Not everyone sees me as just a body. That distinction appears to be a peculiar trait of you and Gina.'

'A job?' he sneered. 'We both know as what. But I hate to tell you, *cara*, distinguished as he is, he cannot afford you.'

She was about to snap back with the truth, but they had reached the foyer and a member of staff arrived with their coats.

What the hell? Why bother to explain? It wouldn't make a blind bit of difference to the way Max felt about her. He saw her as an experienced woman with dozens of lovers, thanks to Abe, and tonight there was no longer any point in telling him the truth. Because she no longer cared.

She looked at him, tall, dark and stony-faced, as he held out the rich sable coat—another one of his presents she really didn't appreciate. He had dismissed her arguments on wearing real fur in his usual autocratic manner. Venetian women in winter *all* wore fur. Maybe he was right, and she had actually seen children in fur coats, but it didn't make her like it—or him, she thought as he helped her to slip it on, keeping his arm around her shoulders.

It was a miserable night—a thick fog had descended, along with drizzling rain. Luckily the launch was waiting, and she stepped on board, shrugging off Max's restraining arm, and walked down into the small cabin and sat down.

She heard Max talking to Diego and hoped he would stay on deck. Sophie let her head fall back and closed her eyes; she could feel the beginnings of a tension headache—hardly surprising, under the circumstances. It was impossible to believe she had left the house with a smile on her face a few short hours ago, confident she could handle her relationship with Max, fooling herself that they got along well and he was genuinely beginning to care for her. Only for the evening to turn out an unmitigated disaster. It had opened her eyes to a reality she didn't want, couldn't accept, and made her realise she had been in danger of succumbing to living in a fool's paradise. Well, no more….

Rising from the seat, she exited the cabin. Max was leaning against the roof, with Diego at the wheel. Diego's head turned. 'Well timed, Signorina Sophie.' He grinned at her as he swung the boat in to the landing stage.

She smiled back, ignoring the looming figure of Max. It was Diego's hand she took as she stepped off the boat, and she didn't wait but ran up the steps and into the house. She slipped the sable from her shoulders, not caring where it fell, and she didn't stop until she reached her bedroom and closed the door behind her. She kicked off the killer heels and, withdrawing her earrings, walked to the dressing table and dropped them in a box. The necklace quickly followed. She stepped out of her dress and slipped on a towelling robe. With the outward signs of Max's ownership gone, she heaved a deep sigh of relief.

She picked up a sliver of lace that in Max's opinion passed for a nightgown and, walking into the bathroom, locked both doors. Now all she had to worry about were the inward signs of his ownership, and she had a nasty suspicion they would be a lot more difficult to deal with. She pulled on a shower cap, had a quick shower, twisted her hair into one long braid over her shoulder and slipped on her nightgown and robe again. Unlocking both doors, she walked back into her bedroom—only to find Max standing there, a glass of whisky in his hand.

'Running scared, Sophie?' Max fixed her with an unwavering glare. 'Or an act of defiance?'

'Neither,' she said flatly, ignoring the angry tensing of his jaw as she met his gaze. 'Just an overwhelming desire to be clean after an evening spent with you and Gina.'

'What the hell do you mean by that?' he demanded, and she shivered, her stomach muscles knotting at the anger evident in his dark eyes.

Max saw her tremble, and for a moment the fury inside him subsided, his eyes narrowing astutely on her flushed but stern face. Thinking back, he recalled other times when Sophie had made remarks about Gina. Given that Sophie had only met her a couple of times, it made no sense. He drained the glass of whisky and crossed to put it on the bedside table before walking back to stare down at her.

'Tonight you made your distaste plain the moment we arrived. I can understand that the thought of cancer scares you—I know it does a lot of people,' he prompted. 'But what have you got against Gina?'

Sophie paled. Good, Max thought savagely, he was on the right track. 'I want the truth, and I am in no mood for any more of your sly innuendos.'

Pale with fury at his sanctimonious comment about understanding her fear of illness, Sophie threw him a venomous glance—the only sly person around here was Max, and she had had enough.

'Oh, please,' she drawled, her eyes spitting fury. 'What do you take me for? An idiot? You and your sainted stepsister Gina have been having an affair on and off for years and everyone knows it.' A short laugh of derision left her lips. 'My God, she flung herself into your arms tonight and the pair of you kissed like long-lost lovers. It was disgusting.'

'*Basta*,' he roared, and she took an involuntary step backward. But it was futile. In one lithe stride Max had narrowed the space between them. Steely hands caught hold of her arms and hauled her hard against him, his dark gaze sweeping over her swift and savage.

'Oh, no, you don't,' he grated, and his eyes narrowed as she began to struggle. 'Stop!' he commanded furiously, and his fingers bit into her soft flesh.

'You're hurting me.'

'Right at this moment I don't damn well care,' he swore. 'I would flatten *any* other person without the slightest hesitation for even *implying* what you have just said,' he revealed harshly.

Sophie stared at him defiantly. 'You can't face the truth, that's your trouble.'

Max saw the determination and conviction in her eyes and realised she actually believed what she was saying. For once he was speechless. He heaved in a strangled breath. 'You actually believe I...' He couldn't say it, and with a shake of his head he shoved her away. 'That is some sick opinion you have of me.'

'Not an opinion. Fact.'

'Fact—Gina is my stepsister, period. She kissed me because she was pleased to see me—a quite common occurrence in my culture. As for anything more, that is only in your head.' He looked at her lovely face, saw the childish braid over her breast rise and fall as she took a deep breath and wondered how anyone so beautiful could harbour such evil thoughts. Maybe it was jealousy. For some reason that did not seem so bad, if a bit extreme. 'If you're jealous—'

'Jealous?' Sophie cut him off. 'Don't flatter yourself—

and don't bother lying.' She swallowed nervously. 'I was there, remember? Seven years ago. The stupid teenager with the enormous crush on you. Marnie warned me about you. She told me about your legion of women and I refused to listen. She even showed me a magazine article about you, with photographs of some of them. Finally she told me about your affair with Gina, *and* the fact that your father didn't approve of the relationship. But I still refused to believe what kind of man you were. I was the dumb kid you seduced and asked to marry because you thought I might be pregnant.'

Her eyes filled with anger. 'The idiot who believed you—until I walked through the maze and heard you and Gina talking about me. To give Gina her due, at least *she* said you had to tell me about her if you really intended marrying me. I heard you both discussing whether I was worldly enough to accept the situation—and you call *me* sick?'

Sophie didn't see the colour drain from his face; she was swamped by memories she had tried to suppress. But no longer. 'What a joke!' She laughed—a raw sound. 'And when Gina asked why you were marrying me your response was a real eye-opener—*because you were careless and I might be pregnant*. Then came her descriptive account of how life would be for the pregnant bride, with a husband who took off at regular intervals to stay overnight with his lover and then came back too tired to make love to his dumb wife.

'My God, it was a revelation,' she spat at him. 'And how could I ever forget your comment that it had only been a couple of days, and with luck you wouldn't have to tell me

anything at all. Well, you got lucky,' she mocked bitterly.
'I wasn't pregnant. And I had no intention of joining a
three-way relationship then and I haven't now. So don't
try and fob me off with Italian culture or any other excuse.

'As I walked round into the centre of the maze I heard
you say you loved each other, and I found you in each
other's arms. Last month in Rome I found her medicine
in the en suite bathroom cabinet, along with signs of your
other women.' She paused, then added with a shake of her
head, 'The only thing that amazes me is why Gina puts up
with you. I have no choice—as you so often remind me.
You are a despicable excuse—' She raised her eyes, and
for a heart-stopping moment she thought he was about to
strike her. His face was contorted with rage, and she
shivered at the cold black fury in his piercing gaze.

'Shut up—just shut up.'

Max had listened with a mounting horror that had quickly
turned to red-hot rage. He wanted to grab hold of her and
shake her. He couldn't believe that Sophie, the woman he
had made love to for weeks, had all the time been harbour-
ing these cancerous thoughts about him. No pun intended,
he thought blackly. And that stopped him. His brain rerun-
ning what she had just said, recalling the conversation, the
circumstances at the time, he could begin to see why, fed
by gossip, she had jumped to the wrong conclusion.

'*Dio mio!*' Max curved a hand around her neck. He
could feel the rapid beating of her pulse against his fingertips, and he looped an arm around her waist and hauled
her hard against him. 'You actually believed that rubbish?'
he snarled, his dark eyes sparking with outrage. 'You crazy
fool! You listened to gossip and believed the worst of me.'

'The magazines didn't lie.'

'I was over thirty—of course I had slept with a few women.' His hand tightened on her throat. 'But as for the rest—you got it all wrong in your stupid juvenile mind.'

'I heard you, remember?' Sophie shot back, refusing to be intimidated by the towering proximity of his great body bristling with outraged fury.

'You said you heard everything, but you didn't.'

'I'm—'

'Shut up and listen,' he roared, his hand moving higher to grasp her chin, turning her face to his, forcing her to meet his eyes. 'The day you overheard me talking to Gina we were *not* talking about a three-way relationship. I have never had one in my life. Nor have I ever had anything other than a brother and sister relationship with Gina. Her preference is for her own sex, as it happens—Rosa is her partner. You should have had more sense than to listen to the idle gossip of a middle-aged woman like Marnie.'

'She said it was common knowledge,' Sophie defended, but the revelation that Gina was gay and Rosa her partner…well, it made sense of the odd tension she had felt when they'd all had coffee together. Her voice lacked a little of her earlier conviction as she added, 'She had no reason to lie.'

'In her dreams,' he grated. 'What you *actually* overheard was Gina comforting me as a sister should—because two days earlier I had been told I probably had testicular cancer. At the same time she was advising me, as a doctor, that I couldn't marry you without telling you the truth, because you would be bound to find out when I went for treatment. Is that plain enough for you?'

He studied her face closely and then smiled mirthlessly. 'The reason she is a little restrained around you is because, as a caring professional, she believed from what you said that you wanted no part of me as a sick man or—in your words—the future I had mapped out. She is a serious woman, and she thinks you are beautiful but too superficial. You can't blame her. Her joke tonight at dinner was perhaps a little crass, but from her past experience perfectly valid.'

At the word *cancer* her stomach had plunged, and shock held her rigid. His dark eyes were cold and hard on hers, but she couldn't look away as a dozen conflicting thoughts whirled in her brain. The overriding one being that surely no man, and certainly not such an arrogantly masculine man as Max, would lie about testicular cancer.

But then again it was still hard to believe, given he'd had no problem making love to her years ago. And his sexual prowess in the bedroom certainly had not diminished over the years—quite the reverse.

'Are you sure you were ill?' She stared at him. 'You seemed remarkably fit to me.'

'Yes, I was.' He met her gaze with sardonic challenge and continued. 'But don't worry—I got over it, and I'm fine now.'

She eyed him uncertainly, remembering that conversation on the fatal day *verbatim*. Dear heaven, she had run it through her head over and over again after they'd parted, to remind herself what a bastard he was in the hope it would cure the hopeless love she felt for him. Could she have been mistaken? Max's explanation made a horrible kind of sense. And if Gina was gay, as he said... She saw again Max reaching his hand to her at the end, when she'd told him she was leaving.

'When you asked me to talk with you and Gina, you meant about your illness?'

'Correct. It was that one-track mind of yours that thought otherwise.'

Appalled, she looked at the face only inches from her own. 'You really *did* have testicular cancer?' she murmured.

'Yes,' he said, a curious blankness in his dark eyes, as though he looked through and beyond her to some bad memory.

'Oh, my God!' All the blood drained from her face. 'I'm sorry—so sorry. What must you both have thought of me?' No wonder Gina was offhand with her. And as for Max, the anger she had sensed in him since they'd met again was now easily explained. He wanted her body, but he thought she was heartless. 'If only I had realised...' Green eyes full of compassion fixed on his. She wanted, needed to tell him—what? That she would never have left him? That she loved him? No, she didn't dare. 'If I'd known you were ill I would—' But he cut her off.

'It would have made no difference,' he said flatly. 'It was caught very early, quickly treated, and I've been clear for years. I don't need your pity.' Drawing her closer to him, he slowly ran his hand down from her throat to lightly cup her breast. 'Only your body. That hasn't changed.' For interminable seconds he stared down at her in total silence, then gave a mocking laugh. 'And before you go beating yourself up over it—you were right. I *did* set out to seduce you. I heard the bad news in the morning and took you to bed in the evening to reaffirm my manhood. Apparently it's a common impulsive reaction with most men, according to Gina.'

'Thanks for that,' she snapped. 'Glad to be of service.' From feeling heartsick and sorry, she was suddenly angry—and yet aroused as his hand slipped inside her robe.

'My pleasure,' Max said sardonically. 'So we both made a mistake years ago? It doesn't matter—I much prefer what we have now.'

She stared at him with huge pained eyes. She knew exactly what he meant; he had never wanted a teenage wife—or any other kind—he much preferred a mistress. Nothing had changed...including her devastating physical awareness of him. But it wasn't enough, would never be enough for her....

As if he knew what she was thinking, he gave her a slight arrogant smile, his head lowering.

'No...' she murmured. 'No,' she said more forcibly, and, shoving hard at his chest, she twisted. But he quieted her by capturing her hands in his and folding his arms around her.

'Yes,' he mocked.

She flung her head from side to side, but he backed her to the bed, and then she was falling.

His impressive body came over her and his mouth covered hers. She tried to keep her lips sealed, but he circled them with his tongue and bit gently, until with a helpless sigh she opened for him. He clasped her head in his hands and kissed her with a deep, possessive passion that stole the breath from her body.

'Forget the past,' he murmured, and stripped off her robe, his dark gaze skimming over her thinly covered slender body. 'The present is all I am concerned about.'

'But—' she started, but he bent his head and kissed her again and again, until she groaned with pleasure. And when he left her for a moment, to strip off his clothes, she simply watched with dazed, hungry eyes. He came back to her and divested her body of the scrap of lace to cover it with his own.

Much later, lying in his arms as the aftermath of passion subsided, Sophie hugged him close and stroked her hands up his chest, her earlier burst of defiance forgotten as she thought of what he must have gone through. Her heart filled with love and compassion for what he must have suffered.

She murmured, 'I am truly sorry you were ill, Max.'

A barely stifled oath left his lips, and abruptly he rolled off her and the bed. 'I told you—I don't need your mawkish sympathy,' he said coldly. 'I never did.' And he left.

CHAPTER ELEVEN

SOPHIE GOT OUT OF BED late the next morning after a restless night, and felt sick. Hardly surprising: the enormity of her mistake about Max and Gina haunted her. Dear heaven, what a fool she had been at nineteen—and she wasn't much better now. Because, being brutally honest, last night, with the original cause of mistrust between them resolved, she had nursed a secret hope that he might grow to love her as she loved him. Well, he had certainly disabused her of that notion. When was she going to learn?

He was a giant of a man in every way—enormously rich, successful and supremely confident in his abilities to defeat anything or anyone who stood in the way of what he wanted. A silent laugh escaped her. Given his stamina in the bedroom, not even cancer had dared dent his virile power. But he had not stayed in her bedroom last night, and that said it all....

It was Friday; he had probably left for Rome. It crossed her mind to wonder whether he would tell Gina the truth, and realised bitterly it didn't really matter. She was still the mistress and would never be anything more.

She dressed and went down to the kitchen, and poured

herself a cup of coffee from the pot on the stove. She took a sip as Maria came bustling in through the back door.

'That is my job. You should have rung,' Maria scolded her. 'Now, what would you like for breakfast?' And she told her to sit down.

Sophie pulled out a chair and sat down, a bitter smile curving her lips. Everyone had a job but her, and being a lady of leisure was really not her scene. Even the coffee tasted bitter, she thought, but drained it down to the dregs. Unless she did something about the sybaritic lifestyle Max had ordained for her, she was in danger of becoming bitter through and through.

She picked up a banana from the fruit bowl in the centre of the table and rose to her feet. 'Don't bother, Maria, this will do,' she said, and left the kitchen to run back up to her bedroom.

She found the card Professor Manta had given her....

The revelations of last night had changed nothing—except now she knew what Max had really thought of her when they had met up again. Not only had he seen her as a promiscuous woman with a string of lovers, but also as the kind of heartless girl who would walk away from sickness. Her heart ached to think of him suffering, but he had told her quite bluntly he didn't want her sympathy. More chilling, he had also told her what deep down inside she had always known: he had deliberately seduced her years ago, simply to confirm his masculinity when it was threatened.

He didn't want her caring or her compassion. There was nothing more to do except play out the charade of being his mistress until he tired of the sex. And, going on his past record, that shouldn't be long.

But in the meantime she had had enough of bowing to his every order. She sat on the end of the bed and took out her cellphone to dial Professor Manta's number. When she rang off, she had made an appointment to meet him outside the school.

Much to Diego's annoyance, she flatly refused to use the launch, insisting she was going out on her own and wanted to try the *vaporetto,* the public transport. Before he could stop her she left.

The sense of freedom was exhilarating. She met Professor Manta, and after a short interview with the principal of the school accepted the job of teaching two mornings a week until Christmas.

Professor Manta insisted on buying her a coffee at Florian before he had to leave for his hospital clinic, and that was where Max found her....

Last night Max had been furious when he'd discovered the depths of depravity Sophie thought him capable of. But, rather than discuss the rage and resentment burning inside him, he had swept her into bed and made passionate love to her—the only sure way he knew they could communicate.

Even in his wildest days he had never kept two women at the same time. He had demanded fidelity in his relationships for however long they lasted. His affair with Berenice at university had taught him that, after he'd discovered she had slept with half of his friends as well as him.

But this morning, in the early light of dawn, his anger fading, he had finally begun to think straight. He had walked back into Sophie's bedroom, determined to talk to her, but she'd been sound asleep. He'd clasped the sheet and pulled it down, intending to wake her, but had stopped. She'd looked so precious, with her knees tucked up like a baby to her stomach, the childish braid falling over her shoulder and across her breast, and he hadn't had the heart to waken her.

He'd watched her for a long time and realised he had no right to be angry with her. She had been young and innocent. Because of his wealth and lifestyle he'd always been the subject of gossip. It had never bothered him, but to an impressionable young girl it must have been a cause for insecurity. A half-heard conversation and she had leapt to a conclusion based on that gossip. But he was older and wiser, and should have known better. He should have insisted on telling her the truth, made her listen, but instead, because of his own problem, uppermost in his mind, he had told her he never wanted to set eyes on her again.

His perception of her as heartless had coloured the way he had treated her over the last few weeks, and he wasn't proud of his behaviour. He had left her sleeping this morning with one thought in his head—to try and make it up to her.

With that in mind he had given Maria strict instructions that she wasn't to be disturbed, and had spent two hours in his study, clearing up some work. He'd called Rome, and the hospice he helped out at every Friday, and told them he couldn't make it. Then he'd made an appointment with his lawyer for lunch, intent on having the humiliating agreement Sophie had signed destroyed. That done, he hoped maybe they could start again. Finally he had hotfooted it to the jewellers. He wanted to buy her a present; he wanted to surprise her....

But it was he who was surprised. Max stood in the shadow of the buildings for a while and simply watched. She was sitting outside the coffee house sipping coffee and smiling at Professor Manta. Elegant in a mulberry-coloured trouser suit, her silken hair loosely tied back with a velvet ribbon, her face delicately made-up, she looked relaxed and happy.

His hand turned over the small velvet box in his pocket. He was going to surprise her all right. Not with a gift, but with his presence. He had been an idiot to think differently of her, but that did not mean he was going to give up what he had got. She was *his* very sexy mistress, and at the minute a disobedient one. He was damn sure he wasn't going to lose her to some old professor. Straightening up, a look of grim determination on his face, he walked across the square.

'Sophie. I didn't expect to see you here this morning.' He saw her head lift and a guarded look come into her eyes.

'Max what a surprise. I thought you had gone to Rome. You always do on a Friday.'

He barely had his temper under control after the shock of seeing her with the professor. But he saw she was nervous, her hands clenched and twisted in her lap, and he thought, *You have a damn good right to be.*

'Obviously not,' he drawled. 'I have a luncheon appointment with my lawyer.' He turned to Professor Manta. '*Buongiorno, Professore*,' he said, and, indicating a chair, '*Permesso*?'

'*Prego*,' the professor said, and stood up. 'How is the hospice going these days? Still expanding?' he asked Max.

'Yes,' Max said shortly.

'Good work.' Patting Max on the back, he added, 'I have to leave now. I'll give you the pleasure of escorting Sophie home. You're a very lucky man. I can't tell you how grateful San Bartolomeo is to have secured her services. *Arrivederci*.'

Max looked at Sophie for a long, silent moment. 'Explain.'

Sophie drew in a shaky breath. Dressed in a charcoal-grey business suit, and a paler grey shirt and tie, he looked tall, dark and austere—and decidedly dangerous. He was staring at her with cold dark eyes, but she refused to be intimidated.

'I told you. Professor Manta asked me if I was interested in a job.' She gave him a sweetly cynical smile. 'Teaching languages at his grandsons' school—San Bartolomeo. They need someone to fill in for a language teacher who is on extended sick leave until Christmas.' She picked up her coffee and drained the cup. 'I called him this morning and said I was interested. We have just been to see the principal. I start work next week, Tuesdays and Thursdays. Is that okay with you, oh lord and master?' she mocked.

He was taken aback by her vehemence, but he couldn't really blame her after what he had implied last night about the professor. The man actually had offered her a job. He wondered what else he had got wrong about her. But he wasn't about to let her get away with openly defying him. 'Where was Diego while all this was going on? I told you not to leave the house without him. You deliberately disobeyed my orders.'

She pushed back her chair and stood up. 'He is probably at your house, where I left him. As for your orders—I forgot,' she said lightly. 'Now, I am going to catch the *vaporetto* and return—if *that* is okay with you?'

His face grim, he got to his feet and grasped her arm. 'Such meekness. But I will escort you back, and we will discuss your idea of working later.'

'There is nothing to discuss. I have accepted the job at San Bartolomeo.'

'You already have a job. Me,' he reminded her succinctly. 'You also have credit cards and a generous allowance.'

'A salary, don't you mean?' Sophie heard herself snipe, very conscious of Max's steely grip on her arm as they walked to the landing stage.

'Call it what you like, but spend the damn money. Shop, lunch, do what other women do. You don't have to teach a bunch of kids.'

'But I love children—and I hate shopping.'

Max hand tightened on her arm. 'In my experience *every* woman likes shopping with unlimited money. Try it and see,' he drawled cynically.

'Your kind of woman, yes, but not me.' Her head lifted fractionally, and her voice was remarkably calm as she met his dark gaze. 'You really don't know me at all, Max.' The *vaporetto* had arrived and people were disembarking. 'Contrary to what you and Gina think for whatever mistaken reason, I *do* care about people. The only reason I stayed at that dinner last night after being the butt of Gina's so-called joke was not because you threatened me but for my mother. She died of breast cancer, and for two years Meg and I nursed her. The only reason I am here now is because I care for my brother Timothy. If you had the least interest in me in any way other than sexual you might have realised that.'

His hand fell from her arm and she saw a muscle jerk in his cheek. He didn't like that, but she was sick of pandering to what Max liked.

'I finally realised last night exactly how you see me. In your mind I am an experienced woman of the world, out for what I can get from any man and without a caring bone in my body. And do you know what really sickens me? Even believing that, you still had no scruples about enjoying my body. So what does that make you?'

Not waiting for a response, she walked on board the *vaporetto*, went inside the cabin and sat down.

A few moments later a stony-faced Max sat down beside her, the warmth of his hard thigh seeping into hers.

'I thought you had a lunch appointment,' she gibed, trying to move along the seat, but she was pressed up against the window already.

'*Non importante*,' he said, with a wave of his hand. 'You and I need to talk.'

'I know your idea of talking. A few brief commands that usually involve me being horizontal,' she said bluntly. 'But you're wasting your time today. Every Friday afternoon Tessa brings her children over. I give them an English lesson and we all have dinner together. My life does not stop when you're not around.'

She looked at him. His starkly handsome face was dark and taut, and she could feel the tension in the long muscular body so close to hers. 'And if you are going to tell me I can't accept the job at San Bartolomeo, forget it. The way I feel at the minute, the thought of working is the only thing keeping me sane. For two pins I would say to hell with you *and* my father and get back to my own life. So don't push it.'

'No, I don't mind you working at San Bartolomeo at all,' Max said swiftly. The very idea of her leaving him was not something he could bear to contemplate.

'Just as well,' she muttered, the wind taken out of her sails. Maybe Max was getting tired of her. That was her next thought. She turned her head and looked out of the window, for some inexplicable reason moisture glazing her eyes.

'This is our stop.' He took her arm and led her off the boat.

'Are you sure?' she glanced around. 'This is not where I caught the *vaporetto*.'

His hand tightened momentarily. 'This is quicker.' And, holding her arm like a vice, he strode forward. She stumbled to keep up with him. He never once slackened his pace, and he almost pulled her up the steps to the house.

'Where is the fire? she asked breathlessly, trying to shake off his hand as they entered the hall.

He stood looking down at her for a moment, towering over her, his eyes glittering with some fierce emotion. 'In me,' she thought she heard him say. But at that moment Diego came dashing from the kitchen.

'*Signor*, you are back.'

'Yes, and I want a word with you.'

With Max's attention diverted, Sophie slipped upstairs to her room. She kicked off her shoes as usual, took off her suit and replaced it with the pink tracksuit she favoured for visiting the gym and hanging around the kitchen with Tessa and the children.

Her stomach rumbled and she realised she was starving;

she had eaten only a banana at breakfast. She had her hand on the door to go back downstairs when suddenly it was flung open. Instinctively she put her other hand to her face and went staggering back against the wall.

'Sophie!' She watched with eyes that were watering as Max dashed into the room.

'You could have broken my nose, you great oaf.' Blinking, she shoved the door back. 'As it is, my knuckles will be black and blue for weeks. Are you raving mad? Have you never heard of knocking?' she yelled, straightening up and rubbing her bruised hand with the other.

She was not aware of the fierce tension affecting Max's tall frame. She was too busy checking out her own; her back wasn't feeling too great after its sudden contact with the wall.

'Yes, I *am* mad—about you,' Max said fiercely, and suddenly he was in front of her, his hands reaching for her, roaming gently over her head and her shoulders, down her arms. '*Dio!* If I've hurt you I will never forgive myself.'

Wide-eyed, Sophie stared up at him and saw such pain, such passion in his dark eyes, her breath caught in her throat. She couldn't believe what she was hearing—what she was seeing.

'I'll call the doctor,' he declared, his hands moving feverishly over her. 'My love, I couldn't bear it if I lost you.'

'What did you say?' she asked, stunned.

The austere, sophisticated mask Max usually presented to the world had cracked wide open, and he looked absolutely frantic.

'The doctor. I'll call the doctor.'

'No—after that,' she prompted, a tiny ray of hope

lighting her heart as she saw his slight confusion. 'Tell me again.' She needed to hear him say *my love* so she could start believing it might be possible.

His hands stopped their urgent search and settled on her waist, his dark eyes holding hers. 'I couldn't bear it if I lost you,' he said, in a voice husky with emotion.

Sophie saw the vulnerability in his eyes and was amazed that Max, her handsome, arrogant lover, could be so unsure of himself.

'I did once, and I never want to make the same mistake again.'

'And why is that?' she asked, hardly daring to breathe, the ray of hope growing bigger and brighter by the second.

Max tensed, his hands tightening on her waist, a flush of colour burning under his skin as he looked at her. 'Oh, I think you know, Sophie.' Even now he had difficulty saying the words. Even when he knew his happiness, his life, depended on convincing the woman in his arms to stay with him. 'My love.'

He had said *my love* again; she had not imagined it. Sophie was suddenly conscious of the erratic pounding of her heart, and it took every shred of courage she possessed to ask the next question. 'Am I really your love, Max?

'Yes.' Max gulped, his eyes burning into hers. 'I love you, Sophie. I know I have given you no cause to believe me, but it is the truth. I love you.' From not being able to say the words, Max suddenly had no trouble repeating them. In fact he would tell her a million times over if he thought it would convince her to stay with him.

It was the answer she had prayed for, and Sophie drew a shaky breath. Only then did she raise her hands to touch him. She ran her fingers through his hair and cradled his head in her palms. 'You love me?' She paused, saw the answer he made no attempt to hide in his dark luminous gaze, and added, 'As I love *you*, Max.'

She finally told him the truth she had held in her heart for years. Because the impossible had happened; Max loved her. Tears of emotion misted her vision, a smile of pure joy that reflected her inner radiance lighting her beautiful face.

'You love me? You really mean that, after all I have done?' he asked roughly, and his doubt squeezed her heart.

'I fell in love with you the first moment I saw you. I still love you and always will.'

Max saw the truth in the glittering green eyes that met his intense gaze.

'Ah, Sophie. I don't deserve you,' he groaned, and kissed her with a deep tender passion. She clung to him and returned the kiss with all the love in her heart. His arms tightened around her and he lifted her off her feet to lay her gently in the middle of the bed. Quickly he shed his clothes, but Sophie was almost as quick pulling off her tracksuit and panties.

Max groaned, falling down beside her and scooping her into his arms. Their limbs entwined, she glimpsed the deep, throbbing desire in the depths of his smouldering eyes as his mouth met hers. She gloried in the hungry passion of his kiss and reciprocated with a wondrous abandon. He loved her, and she cried out his name as his mouth found her breasts, his caressing hands arousing and exploring until her every nerve was taut with quivering, aching desire—and more. Love had freed the hungry yearning inside her. Urgently her hands roamed over his hard muscled body, from his wide shoulders down to lean hips.

'Sophie,' he groaned, and he slid his hands under her back. Frantically she locked her legs around him as he surged into her with a primitive and powerful force that reached to her very core. In a wild wonderful ride, their mingled cries echoed a mutual pleasure of cosmic intensity as they reached nirvana, that joining of the souls with creation as one.

They lay, a tangle of welded bodies, breathless, shuddering and speechless, until Max raised his head to say, 'Sophie, my love,' and kissed her with a tenderness so profound her eyes filled with tears of happiness.

Eventually, as their breathing grew steadier, he withdrew from her, then wrapped her in his arms to cuddle her into his side.

'I thought the first time I made love to you was the most intense sexual experience of my life,' Max said thickly, staring down into her flushed face. 'But now…' He was lost for words. '*Dio*, how I love you.' He gave up and kissed her love-swollen lips, slowly, gently and with aching tenderness. He swept a damp tendril of hair from her brow. 'I know I have treated you abominably in the past, and I also know that if I apologise to my dying day it will not be enough.'

'Shh…it doesn't matter,' Sophie murmured, placing a finger on his lips. 'As long as I know you love me now, that is all that matters.'

'No.' Max took her hand and saw the red knuckles, gently brushed them with his lips. 'You're hurt, and I know

I have hurt you in other ways. I need to talk—to explain.' He dropped her hand and she stroked it teasingly up his chest.

'You're sure about that?'

'I need to talk. And I am not going to give in to temptation again until I have,' he said with a wry smile, and recaptured her hand.

'Spoilsport,' Sophie teased

'Maybe.' He grinned and lay back, his deep, husky voice serious. 'But for too long I have used sex as the only way to communicate with you. Now I am determined to tell you the truth.'

'That sounds ominous.' Sophie pushed up on her elbow to stare down at him and threw her other arm over his broad chest, her fingers stroking through his curling chest hair. 'Are you sure you wouldn't rather do something else?'

'Witch.' He grinned again. 'I know what you're trying to do, but I refuse to be sidetracked.'

'Pity!'

He clasped her hand on his chest. 'I am serious, Sophie.' The determination and the intensity of his dark gaze kept her silent. 'From the minute I first set eyes on you in Sicily I wanted you. But Alex warned me off you; you were too young and under his protection. I accepted that, as up until then I'd preferred mature women who knew the score, not dewy-eyed romantic teenagers.' Sophie stiffened. 'Please don't be offended—I am trying to tell you the truth as I saw it at the time.'

'Okay,' she murmured. She was not pleased to think that

Alex had warned Max off, but it *did* explain Max refusing to touch her at first, and she had to admire his restraint.

'I very quickly realised I couldn't keep away from you. I told myself there was no harm in having a light flirtation with a beautiful girl, and I had no intention of taking it any further. I liked my freewheeling lifestyle. But that night when I took you out to dinner, in the car after, I very nearly… Well, suffice it to say it took every bit of will-power I possessed and then some not to follow you into the chalet and make love to you. I left the next day, deter-mined not to see you again.

'In my conceit, I thought there were plenty of willing ladies around without getting embroiled with a teenager. I even convinced myself that the time wasn't right, but if I bumped into you a few years later it would be okay.'

'That was some conceit,' Sophie could not help saying.

'Yes, I know. But a few days later I was already weak-ening,' he said with a wry smile. 'I went to Russia intend-ing to get rid of my sexual frustration with a lady there. But I didn't. I returned to Rome and made a date with an old flame for that night. I left her at her door, still frus-trated.'

'I'm not sure I like such determination,' Sophie murmured.

'Nothing happened, I swear,' Max said quickly. 'On the Friday morning I went though my personal mail in the office and there was a letter informing me to get in touch with the clinic I had attended earlier for a medical. There was some doubt about a sample I had given. I made the ap-pointment the same morning, and it was then I discovered I might have cancer. I'd already arranged to meet Gina for lunch, and she filled me in on the facts. It was easily treatable, with a very high success rate, and did not necessarily affect a man's virility. But as a precaution I should freeze some sperm just in case I couldn't father a child naturally.'

'Oh, my God! You must have felt terrible!' Sophie said, blinking back the tears pricking at her eyes and squeezing his hand. But he let her hand go. He still wasn't prepared to accept her sympathy, she realised sadly.

'No, what I felt was furious—and scared. I couldn't believe it was happening. From thinking I had all the time in the world, I was wondering if I had any. It seems selfish now, but the one thought in my head was that if I was going to die I was going to make damn sure I had you first. And I ordered the plane to take me to Sicily.'

How like her impulsive, arrogant, but adorable Max, Sophie thought, a husky chuckle escaping her.

'It wasn't funny,' Max chided her. 'When I saw you by the pool all I could think of was making love to you. I suppose I did deliberately seduce you. But when we made love it was the most wonderful experience in my life. Until now.'

Max reached up and tenderly outlined her lips with one long finger, his dark eyes burning into hers. 'I would like to say I knew I loved you then, but l have to admit that afterwards I did wonder if it was a subconscious reaction at the thought of having cancer—a need to prove there was nothing wrong with me as a man. All I do know is that when you lay asleep in my arms I thought I wouldn't mind if you were pregnant. And when I asked you to marry me I did mean it. Later, of course, when Gina arrived, it all fell apart. And now we know why.'

Sophie could understand his uncertainty, but she chose

to believe he had loved her from the start. Raising her hand, she gently stroked his cheek, her green eyes gleaming with love. 'That was my fault. I should have listened to you.'

'No. No, it was mine. I was older and should have explained. Instead I dismissed you as a heartless young girl. I was determined to put you out of my mind and concentrate on getting better. The latter I succeeded in doing quite easily. But forgetting you was not so easy.'

'Good, I'm glad.' She let her hand stroke over his shoulder and moved closer, to stretch one long leg over his thighs.

'Yes, well… I am trying to confess here, Sophie, and you are trying to do something else.' His mobile mouth quirked at the corners. 'And it is not going to work. At least not yet.'

She responded by slumping on top of him, her breasts against his chest. 'Okay, go on.' She wriggled, and he laughed.

'When I saw you again at that dinner, looking so beautiful with Abe Asamov, I saw red.'

'I was never *with* Abe, the way you mean. I spent a summer vacation from university in Russia with his wife and children, teaching them English. He is just a friend,' she explained quickly. 'I hadn't seen him for ages, and he just acted like that for fun.'

'Yes, well, it doesn't matter now.' Max believed her—he had to, for his own peace of mind. 'But at the time I think I went a little crazy. I had been helping out with the hotel business, and your father's name had come up—as you know.' He grimaced. 'I decided it was fate. I should never have forced you into being my mistress, but once I had, and you were so responsive in my arms, I told myself that was all I wanted. Until last night. I stormed from this bed because I didn't want your sympathy. But I came back and watched you sleeping, and knew then that I loved you quite desperately. Because I wanted so much more. I wanted back the love you once said you felt for me.'

'You should have wakened me, then,' Sophie said softly

He smoothed a hand over her cheek and swept back the long swathe of her hair, his dark eyes holding hers. 'No. I was determined not to make mistakes this time. I arranged to meet my lawyer for lunch, to cancel that demeaning contract I made you sign, and then I went out to buy you a present—to surprise you, to ask if we could start again. But you surprised me. I saw you with Professor Manta and I was mad with jealousy.' His lips curved in a self-deprecatory smile.

'But it got worse. I discovered he really had offered you a job teaching, and then came your revelation about your mother, your flat refusal to spend your time and my money shopping, like all the other women I have known.'

She didn't like *all the other women*, but she let it pass. He was hers now.

'I had misjudged you over and over again. You were right when you said I didn't know you at all. I stood for a moment, paralysed with fear, and watched you board the *vaporetto*, certain I was going to lose you. I followed you on board determined to make it my life's work to remedy that and keep you at any cost.'

'You've succeeded,' Sophie said, her voice husky with emotion. That Max, her arrogant, magnificent lover, should bare his heart to her had convinced her beyond a shred of doubt that he really did love her. She looped an arm around his neck. 'If you've finished talking...' she smiled, a slow, sensuous curve of her lips '...can I do what I want now?' And she pressed her lips against his throat, then to the hollow of his shoulder blade, whilst her slender fingers traced his silky chest hair and she teased a hard male nipple.

'It depends what you want,' Max said, on a strangled groan.

Pushing on his chest, Sophie sat up, straddling him. Tossing her head back, her green eyes gleaming, she said, 'I want to make love to you. I always want to; it is just what you do to me.'

Max had never heard, felt or seen anything more seductive in his life. Her beautiful face was flushed pink, her glorious hair falling in a tumbling mass around her shoulders, playing peek-a-boo with her lush breasts, and as for her thighs gripping him...

'Feel free,' he murmured.

In the silence of the afternoon, with the sun pouring through the window, Sophie did just that. She was like a child in a candy shop as she kissed and licked her way down his great torso, tracing his belly button and lower, stroking his thighs, and by the time she was kneeling between them he was painfully aroused. Fascinated, she stroked her hands up his inner thighs.

'I never knew a man could be so...beautiful,' she said, glancing up at his taut, dark face. She grinned a broad, beautiful smile. 'You are perfect.'

For a long moment Max stared at her with the strangest look in his eyes, and then said, 'What about Sam?'

Sophie frowned in confusion. 'What about Sam? I'm going to be her bridesmaid in February,' she murmured.

'*Her* bridesmaid—Sam is a *woman*?' he choked. 'Tell me, Sophie, how many lovers have you had?'

'Well…' She pretended to think as it dawned on her that Max was very definitely jealous, and had been from the minute they'd met again. First Abe, and now Sam. 'Let me see, including you—one.'

He pulled her down to take her lips with his in a fierce, possessive kiss, and then, grasping her thighs, he thrust up into her sleek wet heat in a paroxysm of passion.

Sophie collapsed on top of him, her heart pounding fit to burst as she felt the lingering spasms of their mutual climax in every nerve-ending of her body. With his arm wrapped securely around her, his hand gently stroking her hair, calming her down, she closed her eyes.

'Are you all right?' Max asked.

She heard his huskily voiced question and opened her eyes, looking up at him, a languorous smile curving her full lips. 'Surprised, but never better,' she sighed.

'Surprised… *Surprise*!' he exclaimed, and pushed her away. He leapt off the bed and picked up his trousers.

It *was* time they surfaced, she supposed. Heaven knew what the staff must think. And she swung her legs off the bed—only to see him drop his trousers again.

'Max?' she queried, and to her amazement he fell to his knees and grasped her left hand.

'I almost forgot your surprise.' He opened a velvet box and held up a magnificent emerald and diamond ring.

'Will you marry me? I swear I will love and cherish you to my dying day.'

His starkly handsome face, taut with strain, filled her vision, and tears of emotion flooded her eyes. 'This was my surprise?'

She swallowed the sob in her throat. He wanted to marry her—he had already bought the ring.

'Yes,' he said, and, taking her hand, slipped the ring on her finger. He stood up, pulling her with him. 'Now, all you have to do is say yes.'

'Yes,' she cried, and their lips and hearts met in a kiss like no other—a kiss that was an avowal of love and a promise for the future.

'Are you sure about this?'

Sophie fingered the pearls at her throat, her wedding gift from Max, and glanced up at him with a wealth of love and laughter in her sparkling green eyes. Today was her wedding day, and with her family and friends from England, and Max's family and friends in attendance, they had married, in a moving church service in Venice.

Sam and Gina had been her bridesmaids, and Timothy a pageboy. Gina, on learning of the gossip and the trouble caused by her hiding her sexuality, had come out, and her mother had accepted the fact.

The wedding breakfast had been held in an elegant restaurant near the church, and now they were going home by gondola, to change and adopt a more modern form of transport to fly to Paris for a short honeymoon.

'Trust me,' Max said huskily. He had never seen Sophie look more exquisite, in a long white velvet gown, her magnificent hair loose, entwined with a crown of rosebuds, and a velvet muff decorated with the same flowers on one wrist. She looked like some fey medieval princess and she took his breath away. She already had his heart.

He caught her hand and helped her into the gondola. Sitting down, he drew her to his side. 'It is a tradition that Venetians travel in a gondola on their wedding day.'

'You're not Venetian,' she pointed out teasingly, and a great cry went up from the crowd gathered at the landing stage as the vessel, covered in garlands of flowers, began to move.

'True—but we would never hear the end of it from Diego and Maria if we didn't,' Max offered, looking down at his beautiful blushing bride.

'You're such a pussycat, really, Max Quintano.' Sophie laughed.

'And you, Sophie, are my wife—Signora Quintano,' he said, with pride and heartfelt satisfaction. And he couldn't resist; the kiss in church had not been nearly enough. Closing his arms around her, he kissed her again.

The gondola rocked and the crowd cheered again, but the two locked together heard nothing but the pounding of their two hearts as one.

Much later that evening, after they had consummated their marriage, they lay with their limbs entwined in the huge bed of the bridal suite in a luxurious Parisian hotel, and Sophie gave Max her wedding gift.

'You know you told me Gina insisted you freeze your sperm just in case you couldn't father a child?' She felt him tense and kissed his jaw. 'Well, there was no need. I'm pregnant.'

He grasped her hand and their eyes met, and she was sure she saw moisture in the luminous depths of Max's. 'That's incredible—a miracle. But are you sure? How? When?'

'Well…' She linked her fingers through his and cuddled up to him, secure in his love for her. 'A certain guy walked into my bedroom and laughed at my dolls, and then he made love to me and left for a while. Then later he returned, with a bottle of wine and two glasses and nothing else, and he made love to me again.' She knew the exact moment, and as he remembered his mouth curled in a broad smile.

Max chuckled, and the grip on her hand tightened. 'It must have been all those eyes watching me that made me forget protection.' He drew her to him, the look in his eyes one she knew very well.

'Or maybe I should have mentioned that a couple of the dolls I collected on my travels are fertility symbols.'

He threw back his dark head and laughed out loud. 'Ah, Sophie, *amore mia*, you are truly priceless and all mine—now and for ever.' And he proceeded to show her what he meant, with her enthusiastic co-operation.

HARLEQUIN *Presents*®

Bedded by...
Blackmail
Forced to bed...then to wed?

BOUGHT BY HER HUSBAND
by Sharon Kendrick

For Max Quintano, blackmailing
Sophie into becoming his mistress
was simple—she'd do anything to
protect her family. Now she's
beholden to him, until she
discovers why he hates her....

Dare to read it?

On sale July 2006

www.eHarlequin.com   HPBBB0706

HARLEQUIN®
Presents

The world's bestselling romance series...
The series that brings you your favorite authors,
month after month:

Helen Bianchin...Emma Darcy
Lynne Graham...Penny Jordan
Miranda Lee...Sandra Marton
Anne Mather...Carole Mortimer
Susan Napier...Michelle Reid

and many more uniquely talented authors!

Wealthy, powerful, gorgeous men...
Women who have feelings just like your own...
The stories you love, set in exotic, glamorous locations...

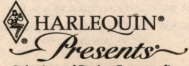

HARLEQUIN®
Presents

Seduction and Passion Guaranteed!

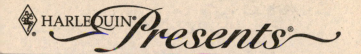

HARLEQUIN *Presents*

Even more passion for your reading pleasure!

UNCUT

Exerience the drama, emotion, international settings and happy endings that you love in Presents novels. But be careful, the thermostat has been turned up a little and these sizzling relationships are almost too hot to handle!

NAKED IN HIS ARMS
by Sandra Marton

When a man is hired to protect a beautiful woman, his solution is to hide her on his private island where the days are hot and the nights intensely passionate....

Feel the heat and read this title today!
On sale this July...

www.eHarlequin.com

HPUC0706

#2547 PRINCE OF THE DESERT Penny Jordan
Arabian Nights

Gwynneth had vowed that she would never become a slave to passion. But one hot night of lovemaking with a stranger from the desert has left her fevered and unsure. Little does Gwynneth know that she shared a bed with Sheikh Tariq bin Salud.

#2548 THE SCORSOLINI MARRIAGE BARGAIN Lucy Monroe
Royal Brides

Claudio Scorsolini married Therese for convenience only. So when Therese starts to fall in love with her husband, she tries to end the marriage—for both their sakes. But Claudio isn't ready to let her go.

#2549 NAKED IN HIS ARMS Sandra Marton
UnCut

When ex-Special Forces agent Alexander Knight is called upon to protect the beautiful Cara Prescott, his only choice is to hide her on his private island. But can Alex keep Cara from harm when he has no idea how dangerous the truth really is?

#2550 THE SECRET BABY REVENGE Emma Darcy
Latin Lovers

Joaquin Luis Sola is proud and passionate and yearns to possess beautiful Nicole Ashton. Nicole reluctantly offers herself to him, if he will pay her debts. This proposition promises that Quin will see a most satisfying return.

#2551 AT THE GREEK TYCOON'S BIDDING Cathy Williams
Greek Tycoons

Heather is different from Greek businessman Theo Miquel's usual prey: frumpy, far too talkative and his office cleaner. But Theo could see she would be perfect for an affair—at his beck and call until he tires of her. But Heather won't stay at her boss's bidding!

#2552 THE ITALIAN'S CONVENIENT WIFE Catherine Spencer
Italian Husbands

When Paolo Rainero's niece and nephew are orphaned, his solution is to marry Caroline Leighton, their American aunt, with whom Paolo once had a fling. Their desire is rekindled from years before—but Caroline has a secret....

#2553 THE JET-SET SEDUCTION Sandra Field
Foreign Affairs

From the moment Slade Carruthers lays eyes on Clea Chardin he knows he must have her. But Clea has a reputation, and Slade isn't a man to share his spoils. If Clea wants to come to his bed, she will come on his terms.

#2554 MISTRESS ON DEMAND Maggie Cox
Mistress to a Millionaire

Rich and irresistible, property tycoon Dominic van Straten lived in an entirely different world from Sophie's. But after their reckless hot encounter, Dominic wanted her available whenever he needed her.